TOMMY TAN AND THE BOWL OF TIME

TOMMY TAN AND THE BOWL OF TIME

Published in Hong Kong by Young Haven, an imprint of Haven Books Ltd
www.havenbooksonline.com

ISBN 978-988-18094-3-8

Cover illustration: Graham Kennedy

TOMMY TAN AND THE BOWL OF TIME

PETER CAIN

YOUNG
HAVEN

Dedicated to my late parents Freda and Stan,
and my late niece Amanda

PROLOGUE

Longsheng region, Southern Provinces, Ancient China

2nd July 650 AD

Prince Wat Su paced up and down the great hall of his palace. He had a problem. A very big problem.

"We must stop him from coming any closer," he roared, pounding his fist in the palm of his other hand.

His trusted advisor, Chou Ping, flinched.

"But how, Excellency?" he murmured. "The warriors in Boon Kong's army are so strong, and with those dragons protecting them, they are practically unbeatable!"

The Prince whirled around. Striding up to Chou Ping, he thrust his face close to the smaller man and said, "You're the magician. You find a way!"

CHAPTER 1

Manchester, England

7th August 2001

Creeeak. Tommy froze and whirled around.

"Sssshhh," he hissed. "I don't want Mum and Dad to know we're up here!"

"Okay, okay," John whispered back.

Tommy was about to say something else when he heard Mrs Tan coming along the corridor. Impatiently, he beckoned John to hurry inside, and quietly pulled the attic door shut behind them.

There was no electricity and what light there was came from two very grimy skylights, which looked as if they hadn't been opened or cleaned for years. Tommy pointed to a far corner. "There they are!" he said.

As John's eyes grew accustomed to the half-light, he could see about six or so large trunks, with thick leather straps tied round them. They reminded him of pirate treasure.

"Wow! What's inside?"

"Things my grandma brought from China when she came

here years ago."

"Can we have a peek?" asked John, his heart starting to race with excitement.

"Sure," said Tommy. "That's why we came up here!" Carefully they made their way over the beams that jutted out of the floor at regular intervals. Every careful movement disturbed the dust of years, which made their noses itch and their eyes water.

As soon as they reached the first trunk, they each started tugging on a strap. Untouched for decades, the straps creaked, complained and refused to budge. However, the boys persisted until finally, first one, and then the other, came undone. They tackled the huge metal clasps next. They were rusty, but luckily there were no locks on them, so with a bit of pulling they managed to prise them open.

Getting up, John stretched. "Nearly there!" he said. "Why don't you grab that side and I'll pull on this side. Ready? One, two, three!"

Gritting their teeth, they heaved on the lid with all their might. The hinges too were very rusty, and gave out terrible groans. But then slowly and with much protest the hinges gave up the fight and let them raise the lid.

The sight that greeted them wasn't very inspiring. The contents seemed to consist of old clothes, which had a strange spicy, musty smell, along with some cracked vases, bowls and ornaments.

"Try not to make too much noise," whispered Tommy, hearing his grandma coughing in the room below.

"I'm not making any more than you!" retorted John, pulling a face. Bending over the trunk again, they both made renewed efforts to be as quiet as they could, as they replaced everything more or less as they'd found it.

Slowly, they inched their way across the beams until they reached the next trunk. This trunk, they both knew instantly, was something special. Even in the poor light, they could see that the workmanship was far more intricate. There were very detailed carvings on the body of the trunk, showing warriors fighting with fearsome-looking dragons, and towards the bottom was a border pattern of what appeared to be pandas. Even the clasps were covered in intricate patterns, which must have taken a skilled craftsman many hours of work.

"Look at this!" hissed John, barely able to contain his excitement.

"Wow," said Tommy, "this must be the trunk Grandma told me about. The one that belonged to my ancestors." John looked up at Tommy and grinned.

"What's so funny?" asked Tommy.

"When I listen to your Lancashire accent, I almost forget you're Chinese," laughed John. The boys shared a smile and then turned back to the trunk.

This time, when they unfastened the straps, the leather slid from the buckles smoothly, as if they'd only been fastened the day before. The clasps were like new, with not a trace of rust or mould. The boys exchanged glances, raising their eyebrows at each other.

"Ready? One, two, three," Tommy whispered, and both of them pulled on the lid as hard as they could. Inside the case was a layer of old newspapers; they carefully removed them. Underneath were some elaborately embroidered dresses and jackets. The colours were vibrant even in the half-light.

Rich, dark reds with luscious greens and shimmering blues greeted their incredulous eyes. The embroidery was amazing, with plants and dragons intertwining in a magical and skilful display of inventiveness.

"These must be silk," said Tommy. "Feel this, it's so smooth and shiny." Under the dresses were a pair of shoes made of embroidered silk, which Tommy also placed on the paper.

Beneath the shoes were yet more bowls and vases of delicately coloured porcelain, which even their untrained eyes could tell were something special. Right at the bottom of the trunk, tucked away in a corner, was a parcel of cloth. Tommy carefully took it out and unwrapped it.

Inside was a bowl, similar in shape to the ones that the Tan family used to eat from, but different. It was more delicate, almost translucent, and the decoration was far finer.

The inside and outside surfaces of the bowl were covered with small figures, which reminded John of the decoration on vases he'd seen in Chinatown. On the base of the bowl were some Chinese letters.

Tucked in the cloth, alongside the bowl, was a pair of elaborate old ivory chopsticks, decorated with gold and mother-of-pearl. As he lifted the bowl from its resting place, Tommy saw that there was also an old parchment, folded carefully into four.

Carefully, he lifted and unfolded the parchment, which had a slightly rough feel, and a strange almost animal-like smell. It appeared quite strong though, and despite some resistance, opened out so the boys could see the faded script within.

"Can you read that?" John asked Tommy.

Tommy shook his head, "I don't know how to read

Chinese."

"Why don't we ask your parents?"

"*No!*" said Tommy firmly. "They mustn't know we've been up here."

"I'd love to know what they were used for," said John. "They look far too good to eat with."

As he spoke, John became aware that his legs had become both numb and painful. "Ouch, I've got pins and needles," he groaned. Without thinking, he tried to stand up, but as he rose, he hit his head on the sloping roof and pitched forward, grabbing at his friend to try and steady himself.

Tommy, who had been perched on a beam, fell heavily backwards onto the thin plasterboard when John grabbed him. A moment later John landed on top of him, and their combined weight sent them crashing right through the floor of the attic.

Mrs Tan had been trying to coax her mother to drink a little weak tea in the bedroom below, when there was a loud cracking noise from the ceiling. She jumped, dropping the teacup, and watched in disbelief as first her son's arm, then head, appeared through the widening hole in the ceiling above the foot of the bed.

She was left speechless when he was joined a split second later by John's head. Alerted by the racket, Mr Tan ran into the room to see a pile of broken plasterboard on the floor and a cloud of dust spreading gracefully over the entire scene. His wife and mother-in-law were staring in open-mouthed amazement at the two boys, hanging upside down from the ceiling.

CHAPTER 2

Longsheng region, Southern Provinces, Ancient China

12th July 650 AD

Prince Wat Su's men gave an ear-piercing battle cry as General Lu Shen shouted the command to attack. The troops that had been waiting on both sides and to the rear of Boon Kong's army, rushed forward with blood-curdling yells. At the same time, mounted troops galloped full tilt towards the wall of raised shields at the front of the enemy army.

Victory seemed certain, as the enemy were far outnumbered, but the general's satisfaction soon turned to dismay. No matter how they tried, the general's soldiers could not injure any of Boon Kong's men. Time after time, the swords, daggers and lances carried by Lu Shen's troops bounced off the strange-coloured armour Boon Kong's men wore.

Unfortunately the armour the Prince's men wore was not as strong, and many were killed or hurt. Alarmed, the general called off his troops.

Several days later, Lu Shen returned to Prince Wat Su's palace to give his report. There were several field commanders present, together with Chou Ping. They fell silent with anticipation as Lu Shen strode in and bowed deeply to the Prince, his noble features twisted with grief and shame.

"Excellency, I have failed you and will give up my post as general."

"Don't talk that way!" snapped Wat Su. "Everybody knows you're not to blame, it's the strange armour they have. We have to find a way of getting past it!"

Chou Ping nodded.

"The only weak spots they seem to have are the eyes, the back of the neck and the legs. If we could train archers to hit these spots, we may be able to disable some of them."

"That would be helpful," agreed Wat Su.

"There is something else you should know," ventured Lu Shen. "Pandas. Boon Kong has ordered his men to trap any pandas his men come across, and ship them back to his stronghold in the north."

"This is hardly a matter of concern," snarled Chou Ping.

"It is," insisted Lu Shen. "He's captured so many there are hardly any left in the wild. What's more, he barely feeds the pandas, and works them to death in his mines."

Chou Ping looked thoughtful. "Now I remember," he said. "The gods in Heaven hold a very special place in their hearts for pandas." Lu Shen nodded. Turning to the others, Chou Ping continued, "You probably don't know that many years ago, the God of the Clouds was cast out from Heaven. He'd just had one of his many squabbles with the other gods, and had caused the God of the Sea to come crashing to Earth and badly injure himself."

"I do seem to remember something of the sort," muttered Prince Wat Su, "but what has this to do with what is happening now?"

"Well, Excellency," said Chou Ping, "the pandas found the God of the Sea, and nursed him back to health, so he was able to return to Heaven. Because of this, the pandas have always been specially regarded by the gods. So much so, that if they were ever allowed to die out, the gods have sworn to punish the Earth for allowing it to happen."

Wat Su looked even more downhearted. "What on earth are we going to do?" he asked the others. "We shall all be destroyed if we can't stop Boon Kong."

CHAPTER 3

Manchester, England

18ᵗʰ August 2001

The week after the trunk incident, John's family went on holiday in Devon in the south of England. Before they left, John visited the Tans, to say goodbye. Tommy took him to the kitchen at the rear of the family's takeaway shop.

"This is my reward for going into the loft!" said Tommy, pointing to the mountain of washing-up his parents had left for him to do.

"I'm really sorry," said John. "I wish I could help you, but we're off in a minute."

"I can't use my computer for two weeks, and I've got to keep an eye on Grandma too," said Tommy miserably.

"My dad was pretty mad too. In the beginning they said I couldn't go on holiday, but Auntie Ena couldn't or wouldn't look after me, so they said I could," said John. He realised he'd got off very lightly compared with his friend.

Just then they heard Tommy's parents coming down the stairs. "Quick, you'd better go," said Tommy. "You're not exactly popular round here."

"Okay," said John, "see you when I get back, and don't work too hard."

"Don't worry about me … You go and have a great time," said Tommy, his voice laced with bitterness. They could hear Mr and Mrs Tan just round the corner, so John left hurriedly, closing the shop door noiselessly behind him.

The trip down to Devon was long and tiring, with road works every few miles on the motorway. Like every year, Mr Cresswell, John's father, had hired a car to take them all down. As usual, he produced a well-worn CD called Girl Singers of the Sixties and inserted it into the player. And, as usual, both John and Joan—who had grown up with the songs— sang loudly along with all the tracks, which made both parents crack a smile, even though they were still hopping mad with John for the trouble he had caused.

By the time they finally arrived at Tidlington, a small, secluded village on the south Devon coast, it was quite late in the day. They collected the keys to the holiday cottage from the owner of the village pub and made their way there. The sight of the small, latticed windows and the roses climbing up the porch made everyone feel better.

Things were quickly unpacked, and Mrs Cresswell soon had a pot of tea made.

"Can Joan and I go to the beach before it gets dark?" John asked his father.

"I've a good mind to keep you shut in the bedroom the whole time we're here!" replied his father, "after all the trouble you've caused."

"Oh, let him go Dad, otherwise I won't be able to," whined Joan.

"Very well then, but you're not to go near the water, and you're to come back as soon as it starts to get dark, do you both understand?" Result, thought John, hiding his grin. Little sisters did have their uses after all!

As they had driven that way earlier, John and Joan knew that the route to the beach would take them past a rather neglected looking café, a small sub-post office that sold cheap gifts, a fish and chip shop, a general store and a second-hand bookshop. There was also a small butcher, greengrocers, and the pub, which was called The Smugglers. They hurried along the narrow uneven pavements, sniffing the salty tang in the air, surprised to find the streets empty. There were a few elderly couples dressed in various shades of tan and brown, strolling around in their sensible walking shoes, enjoying the remnants of a lovely day.

There was also a young family: one parent handling a pushchair, the handles festooned with plastic bags heavy with shopping, while the other attempted to control the boisterous older children who darted between the elderly people as they made their rather uncertain way down the narrow street. All the while the delicious smell of fish and chips floated in the air, making John and Joan very aware that it been several hours since they had eaten anything.

As they passed the bookshop, John glanced in. The window, which was quite dirty, was covered with a yellow plastic film to protect the things inside the shop from the sun's rays. John didn't notice the state of the glass, as he was dazzled by the sheer variety of books within. Although they were not very artfully displayed, he found himself drawn to the hotchpotch pile, which had a book about the Second World War next to a book on Chinese art. Within the darkened interior, were seemingly endless shelves full of books.

John's eyes returned to the book on Chinese art in the window. He made a mental note to come back again when the shop was open.

It only took them a few minutes more to get to the beach, which was almost deserted. The tide was a long way out, and the low sun glinted invitingly on the wet sand, and sparkled on the distant sea. There were patches of seaweed here and there on the sand, and the fresh, clean smell was overpowering.

A man walking by with his dog gave them a friendly wave, which they returned.

Joan found it all irresistible. She tugged her brother towards the concrete ramp that led onto the sand.

"Come on!" she yelled.

"Okay," said John, "but we can't stay for too long; I don't want to upset Dad again." A quarter of an hour passed quickly. John decided that it was time to go home, and had to remove a violently-protesting Joan from what he called her 'sand-houses'—having decided that they weren't really grand enough to be called 'castles'.

Back at the cottage they found their parents relaxing in front of the television, and a supper of fish and chips waiting in the oven. With cries of delight, John and Joan wolfed down their meal and set about enjoying the first evening of their holiday.

The next morning, John, in the deepest of deep sleeps, was gradually wakened by a shrill, insistent noise that gently filtered through his brain until he could no longer make sense of it in his dream. At this point he woke and realised that he could hear birds outside the window.

The sunshine streaming through the curtains made him feel happy. He left his room, half tiptoeing, half dancing along the landing to Joan's room. She was already awake and dressed, and seemed as happy as John was.

"Why don't we make Mum and Dad breakfast in bed?" suggested Joan. John was feeling so good he couldn't help but agree. Not only would it help put him back in their good books, it might also persuade them to help him buy that book he'd seen.

Mr and Mrs Cresswell were woken by the smell of cooking bacon and toast. They couldn't hide their delight and pride when the children appeared, balancing cornflakes, bacon, eggs, toast and tea rather precariously on a large tray they'd discovered in the kitchen.

"Can we go to the shops while you get dressed?" asked John.

"Okay, then," said his father. "Get me a paper at the same time."

Two sets of footsteps rapidly clattering down the stairs and the bang of the front door signalled the siblings' hasty departure. Despite having both just eaten to their fill, their legs propelled them into the village amazingly quickly.

"You get the paper, I just want to look in here," panted John, indicating the bookshop. Surprisingly, Joan did as she was asked without a murmur.

At first the door wouldn't budge, but the sign said OPEN so John pushed a bit harder, until it suddenly flew open, causing the bell to almost ring itself off the wall. Once inside it took John's eyes a few seconds to adjust to the gloomy interior. As he stood there, taking in shelf after shelf of books on all manner of subjects, a voice broke into his wonderment.

"What the devil d'yer want?" it said, a cross between a whine and a snarl. It seemed to have come from behind the curtain of beads that hung over the rear exit to the shop.

"Sorry," shouted John, "but the door was a bit stiff. I didn't mean to push it that hard." A thin man in his fifties appeared through the curtain. His features looked as if they'd never been asked to form a smile, and when he spoke he revealed a set of yellow and black teeth, which reminded John of his father's friend's ferrets.

The man's clothes were dirty, but looked as if they might have been expensive when they were new. His shirt-collar was worn through and the cuffs of his jacket were frayed. What hair he had left was greasy and unkempt. He didn't appear to have shaved that morning and his tie was stained with food he probably consumed over a period of months if not years. He shuffled slightly and had difficulty standing straight.

John's first thought was to make some excuse and get out as soon as possible, but he wanted to see that book.

"Well, what do yer want?" the man repeated.

"Could I please see that book in the window, the one with the Chinese bowl on the cover?"

"You mean the book on Oriental art?" the man sneered. As he turned and reached into the window to get the book, John spotted his sister outside, and pulled a face, grimacing for all he was worth.

Seeing the girl leaning against the window almost helpless with laughter, the man spun around, but was met by the sight of John's back. The boy appeared engrossed in looking at the books on the shelves.

"Here!" he snarled, thrusting the book towards John, "and tell yer sister to behave herself!" Hurriedly, John went outside to tell Joan to take the paper straight back to the cottage.

"Tell them I won't be long," he whispered.

Back in the shop, he found that the man had gone over to a desk at the far end of the room and was opening a pile of post that seemed large for such an out-of-the-way shop. Picking up the book once more, John flicked through it, hoping to find an illustration of the bowl that he'd seen in the Tans' loft, so he could find out more about it.

For some strange reason John had a very precise mental picture of how that bowl and the chopsticks had looked, but, although there were similar bowls, there was nothing exactly the same.

"Thank you for letting me see this," said John, as he handed the book back to the man.

"Mmm," grunted the man, who was by now engrossed in a letter.

John idly ran his fingers along the books that filled every shelf, as he walked towards the entrance. Disappointed that he hadn't found a picture of the bowl, he was a little rougher than he should have been. His action caused one old leather-bound volume to lose a sizable section of its spine, and it tumbled to the floor, which was as dusty as the shelves. Hurriedly, John bent down to pick it up, noticing as he did, that many of the books on that shelf were about the supernatural, witchcraft and black magic.

He gave a little shiver and was on the point of leaving, when something drew his eye to a book on one of the lower shelves. The book wasn't obviously unusual or out of the ordinary, but John felt as if something was drawing him towards it. Intrigued and nervous, he tried to pull it from the clutches of books it was wedged between. With a bit of a struggle it gave up the fight and let John pull it out, sending yet more dust into the air.

The faded label on the shelf read "Ancient Oriental Magic" and the book itself was called *Chinese Magic Potions and Spells*. Looking around to make sure the man wasn't looking, John flicked through the book. About halfway in, he came to a chapter headed "Devices for Spells". A few pages into that chapter was a black and white illustration of the same bowl and chopsticks he had seen in the loft—he was sure of it. The caption under the picture read: "Devices for Transportation".

With his heart racing, and his mouth bone-dry, he concentrated on the illustration, willing himself to look carefully. But no, there was no mistake! He knew he had to have the book.

Apprehensively, he took it to the man at the desk.

"How much is this one please?" he asked.

The man stood up with a look of annoyance on his face, "Isn't it …" he broke off in mid-sentence. "You want this one, do you? It's a bit different from the other one you looked at."

"Yes, it is," agreed John, "but it's got what I want in there."

"And what might that be?" enquired the man, who was

now unconvincingly trying to smile at the boy.

"Oh … nothing much, just something a friend of mine's got."

"Well, seeing as how you're really keen, shall we say seven pounds?" said the man.

Seven pounds! The man might just as well have said seven hundred pounds, or seven thousand pounds. Trying to hide his disappointment, John mumbled, "I'll have to ask my parents, I haven't got that much."

"I'll tell you what," said the man, "you tell me why you want it, and I'll see if I can do you a better price, how's that?"

"No, that's okay. I'll ask my parents, thanks."

The man had now moved from behind the desk, and was standing between John and the door.

"Um, I must get back now," said John as the man moved closer.

"Look, all I want to know is …" Just then the door flew open, setting the bell off again, and a middle-aged American couple half fell into the shop.

"Thanks for your help, 'bye!" shouted John, pushing his way past the man and the tourists.

"Well really," exclaimed the woman, "kids are the same wherever you go!"

"You little …" shouted the bookshop man, not caring that he was scaring his potential customers away from the shop.

John arrived the cottage out of breath. He was unable to compose himself before his mother saw him.

"What on earth's the matter with you?" she asked, alarmed to see her son looking so shaken. "Tell me why you've come in looking like you're being pursued by the hounds of hell."

"Nothing Mum, I just decided to run home, that's all." His mother gave him a very old-fashioned look, which told him that she knew different. Joan, who'd been waiting for him to arrive, stuck out her tongue at her brother and vanished upstairs.

The rest of the fortnight flew by, as holidays usually do. During this time John was woken several times by the same odd dream, in which a strange monkey wearing a tunic and a small helmet appeared. Apart from its clothes, it was clear that the monkey was far from ordinary, because it was able to talk!

Tommy appeared in the dreams too, but John did not recognise where they were. The surroundings were different from anything he'd ever seen before. Strange mountains with jagged peaks and swirling mists loomed over deep, wide rivers and lakes with lush vegetation growing from the banks and up into the lower slopes of the foothills.

To John's horror, the man in the bookshop intruded into his dreams too, his already sour face transformed into a mask of frightening hatred. He was accompanied by several Chinese men wearing long robes and strange headgear, the likes of which John had never seen before. This odd group seemed to be chasing the boys and the monkey, but each time, just when they were about to catch them, John woke up. It was a strange dream, and he could not make any sense of it.

All he knew was he felt very uncomfortable whenever it popped into his head in his waking hours.

CHAPTER 4

Northern Provinces, Ancient China

9th March 633 AD

When he was only ten years old, Boon Kong experienced something that changed him forever. On that fateful day, he had been helping his father in the paddy fields planting rice, but after a couple of hours of backbreaking work in the hot sun, the temptation to wander off had become too great.

He'd waded over to the edge of the field and up into the rocky outcrop above. After climbing up a little way, he'd turned to look back down on the people toiling below, before sitting down and idly picking up a few small stones, which he threw at a bush some way below him.

Most of the stones hit the rock behind the bush with a sharp clack, but the last one landed with a thud, followed by a loud whimper. Intrigued, Boon Kong made his way down from his perch to the source of the sound. It was a terrified panda cub. Most children would have wanted to help the defenceless creature, but not Boon Kong. He had become excited by the prospect of a living target. He'd always had a cruel streak in him, and the anticipation of this very one-sided sport made his day come alive.

Looking around for missiles, he gathered a variety of twigs, stones, and larger rocks, which he rained down onto the terrified animal. Its pitiful cries grew louder with each successive hit. Boon Kong, who was by now really enjoying himself, debated whether to slowly cripple the unfortunate panda or crush its skull with a large rock he could barely lift.

His deliberations were interrupted when, from out of nowhere, a full-grown panda suddenly appeared, attracted by the cries of her offspring. She rushed over to the cub, frantically licking it. Boon Kong realised it was time for him to remove himself from the scene, and started to back away from the enraged mother. He was not quick enough.

Once she was sure that the cub was all right, she turned her attention to the terrified boy who was trying to make his way backwards up the rock face. As she bounded towards him, he turned himself over, scrabbling and hauling himself upwards, driven on by fear.

The panda slipped a few times as she followed him up, and Boon Kong felt relieved. Unfortunately, his relief was short-lived, as she suddenly secured several good paw-holds, and surged up with startling speed, until she reached his legs.

Without warning, she took his left leg in her jaws and sank her teeth in at knee height. He screamed with pain, but had the presence of mind to grab her nose and twist it as hard as he could. The mother released him, and he kicked her in the snout as viciously as he was able. She grunted, slipped, and finally slithered to the bottom of the face with a thud. She went over to the cub and the pair of them vanished over the rock she had first appeared from.

In the meantime, Boon Kong had hauled himself to the top of the rock face—a difficult task, as his left leg was now as good as useless. It took him more than an hour to drag himself back to the village, leaving a trail of blood behind him. A couple of neighbours helped him back to his home where his parents, already upset because he'd vanished from the paddy field, were even more distressed when they saw the state their son was in.

He told them he'd been attacked by the panda for no reason and told them to find it and kill it. Word spread quickly, and soon about a dozen villagers had gathered at his parents' home.

The villagers organised a search the next day, but found nothing. Boon Kong demanded they go out again the following day, but despite his increasingly desperate requests, they refused, as they had crops and animals to attend to.

Slowly, Boon Kong's wounds healed, but his leg was never the same again and he vowed revenge. During the dark nights that followed, he promised himself that one day he would wipe all the pandas from the face of the Earth and would also punish the villagers for not helping to find the panda that had attacked him.

CHAPTER 5

Devon, England

25th August 2001

In no time at all, the holiday was over, and it was time to go home. The Cresswells locked the door of their cottage for the last time and got into the car. As the key had to be returned to the barmaid in the pub, they stopped outside the Smuggler's Arms and Mr and Mrs Cresswell popped in, leaving John and his sister in the car.

When their parents came out of the pub, whom should they be talking to but the man from the bookshop! Oh no, thought John, and dived out of sight onto the car floor. As they came nearer, he heard his mother's parting words.

"So nice to have met you. You must look us up when you're up our way." Getting into the car, she fastened her seatbelt. "What a nice man," she said. "What a shame we didn't meet him sooner."

"Pity about his teeth though," said Mr Cresswell. "They reminded me of Bob's ferrets." At that John burst into laughter.

"Really John, you shouldn't laugh at other people's

appearance," said his mother. "Especially when they've given you a present!"

"A present?" said John, not believing what he was hearing.

"Yes, he told us that you'd been in the shop at the beginning of the holiday and had wanted to buy a book, but you'd never been back in again."

"He wanted a fortune for it," said John.

"Well, he's given it to you, as he said that an interest in other things besides pop music and football were to be encouraged."

John's first thought was, what's the catch? But he said to his mother, "Did I hear you asking him to visit us?"

"Yes, he has friends in Eccersley he visits twice a year, so I told him to look us up next time he's visiting," replied Mrs Cresswell. John suddenly felt cold again, even though the day was quite warm.

The journey back was better than coming down, as there was less traffic and fewer road works, and the family made good time. Mr Cresswell dropped the family off, and then took the car straight back to the hire company. Before she started unpacking, Mrs Cresswell gave John the book, remarking that he seemed to be developing strange interests and that maybe pop music and football weren't so bad after all.

John headed straight upstairs to his bedroom and eagerly flicked through the book until he found the page he was looking for. Sure enough, there was the bowl and the chopsticks, almost identical to the ones he had seen in Tommy's loft. He grinned thinking about how surprised Tommy would be to see the book, then, feeling sleepy, he closed the book and went to bed.

The next day was Sunday. As soon as he woke, John went straight up the road to see Tommy and tell him everything that had happened. When he rang the bell, Mrs Tan came to the door and made it clear that she was not happy to see him.

"Can I just see Tommy for a little while, I promise it won't take long," begged John. Reluctantly, Mrs Tan relented and a few seconds later, Tommy appeared from the back of the shop, looking far more subdued than the last time John had seen him.

"Are you okay?" John asked with concern.

"Grandma died, and my parents think we're partly to blame because of the shock we gave her when we crashed through the ceiling." John could tell that Tommy had been having a hard time of it, as he had dark rings under his eyes and looked very pale. The younger boy opened his mouth, as if to say something else, but the words wouldn't come out. Suddenly, his eyes filled with tears and he started to sob quietly. John, feeling very awkward, took Tommy over to some chairs and made him sit down. Pulling another chair up next to him, John put his arm round Tommy's shoulder. "Listen Tommy," he said, "from what the doctor was saying last time I was here, your Gran didn't have long to live. You're not to blame, do you hear?"

Tommy looked at him and the tears slowly stopped falling as he thought about what John had said.

"That's better," said John, smiling at Tommy, and giving him a clap on the back. "Now, guess what I found when I was on holiday?"

Tommy rubbed his eyes dry. A small smile crossed his face

as he said, "A new ceiling?" John laughed.

"Actually, it's a book. As a matter of fact, it's this one." Proudly, he showed Tommy the book he'd brought with him.

"What the heck is this?" said Tommy, leafing through and looking mystified.

"Give it here," said John, taking it back and finding the page with the illustration on it. "Now do you see?"

"Wow!" said Tommy. "Is it … ? It is, isn't it?" There was a page number printed next to the illustration. The boys eagerly turned to that page.

At the top of the page was a heading, which read: *Commonly Used Devices for Transportation*.

As quickly as they could, they read through the chapter. They were not completely sure if they understood everything, but as far as they could make out, the book was saying that the bowl and chopsticks, if used with the correct words — or 'incantations' as the book called them — would enable a small number of people to be moved from one place and time, to another.

"Do you think it's true?" whispered Tommy in amazement.

"Well, it sounds like the author thought so," answered John. "Can we look at the bowl and chopsticks again to make sure they're the same as in the book?"

"I don't know if we can," said Tommy. "My father's put a lock on the attic door. But we've got to try to get them somehow." Sighing with frustration, John closed the book. Looking at its still dusty cover made John remember the dreams he'd been having, and he turned to tell Tommy about them. To his horror, the Chinese boy turned white.

"Tommy!" John cried. "What's wrong?"

Tommy shook his head. "You won't believe this," he told John. "But I've been having the exact same nightmare. I thought it was because I was upset about Grandma dying."

At first disbelieving, they compared notes very carefully and discovered that every detail seemed to be identical. Tommy could even describe the bookshop man whom he had never even seen! The boys were both excited and shaken by this and tried to find logical reasons for it, but there just weren't any. It was like magic.

CHAPTER 6

Northern Province, Ancient China

21ˢᵗ May 641 AD

After the passage of a few more years, Boon Kong turned eighteen. He still bore the physical and mental scars from the encounter with the pandas. The adults of the village, who noted with some concern that he had become more withdrawn, avoided him, especially on the days when they saw him talking to himself or pounding a fist into his other palm.

The youngsters, however, followed him around and teased him mercilessly. It was only the intervention of an older man that saved a young girl from a savage beating at Boon Kong's hands when he caught her making fun of him.

More and more, Boon Kong became disenchanted with village life. He was sure that he was destined for greater things. He decided to seek out a man who might be able to help him achieve his ambitions. The man that Boon Kong hoped to find was one he'd heard long heard tales about — a hermit who lived in the caves up in the mountains.

By all accounts, he'd been a Holy Man who'd been forced to leave the Temple for abusing his powers and practising the dark arts. He now lived alone, except for two constant companions—a raven and a wildcat.

Boon Kong set out one morning in May. He got up very early, gathered together his few possessions and a little food and drink, and headed up into the mountains to find the hermit. He climbed for days, watching for the raven, which he'd heard acted as the hermit's sentry.

Many days passed without a sign of the bird, but just when he was on the point of giving up, he spotted it, soaring high overhead. Carefully, he watched where it came down to Earth, then, as fast as his damaged leg would allow, he made his way to the spot where he'd seen the bird land. There, by a small stream, he found the entrance to a cave, inside which he could see the flickering light of a fire.

"Who's there?" cried a voice from inside.

"My name is Boon Kong," he replied.

"I've been waiting for you," the voice said.

Boon Kong was taken aback. "How did you know I was coming?" he yelled.

"I know and see many things. This you too will be able to do if you stay and let me teach you," came the reply. Cautiously, Boon Kong entered and found an old man sitting cross-legged in front of a small, flickering fire. He took in the scene as he grew accustomed to the gloom in the cave. By the old man's side was a wildcat, which arched its back and spat at him.

"Don't take any notice of him," the old man said, "he won't hurt you."

He invited Boon Kong to sit down. "Would you like some tea?" he asked. Boon Kong nodded and again the man bade him sit down. As he poured the tea he said, "I knew somebody would come, but only recently had a vision that it would be you. There is no one else in the region who has your focus, or grasp of detail. You are a special young man."

Boon Kong grunted, both embarrassed by the praise, but also happy in the knowledge that his own feelings about himself were justified. "It's good you've come now," the old man said. "I'm getting weaker every day and I don't think that even my most powerful spells will be able to save me soon."

This alarmed Boon Kong. "I was hoping you'd be able to give me some help to become … powerful," he said, not sure whether he was saying the right thing or not.

"Don't worry," said the old man. He started to chuckle, then coughed violently, gasping desperately for breath. "Don't worry, that is the reason you are here. There will be time for me to teach you all you need to know, and more. Great things are expected of you."

Intrigued and excited by this, Boon Kong asked, "What do you mean?"

"Well, my boy, first things first. We shall teach you the basics of Black Magic and Sorcery, and only then shall we send you out into the world to make a name for yourself and gather power, influence and money… for you will need all of these for the next stage of the plan."

"Who is this 'we' you talk about?" asked Boon Kong.

The old man chuckled. "I have an authority who has an interest in expanding his power and influence, but he cannot be seen to do it himself." Boon Kong had begun to wonder what was in store for him, but visions of himself in a grand house with servants, fine clothes and jewellery kept him from fleeing. "You'd better come and sleep now," said the old man. "Tomorrow we will start your education."

He chuckled then coughed painfully once more. He signalled to Boon Kong to move further inside the cave, to a spot that had been prepared for him. It was more basic than the room he had occupied in his parents' house, but Boon Kong was sure that the hardship would be worth it. He fell asleep quite quickly, his head whirling with what he'd just been told.

For a whole year, Boon Kong stayed with the hermit, practising spells and learning all there was to learn. At the end of that time, he possessed all the old man's knowledge. In fact, having learnt to skilfully combine several spells together, he could do more powerful magic than the old man himself. One of his most useful combinations involved treating the metal copper with a defensive spell. The spell had the effect of rendering the copper weapon-proof. The old man was particularly impressed when Boon Kong showed him this.

"Make sure you work out how to produce it in quantity. It will give your troops the advantage."

"What troops?" asked Boon Kong, but the old man would only say, "You will see, you will see."

Not long after this, the hermit died. The God of the Clouds whom Boon Kong had since discovered was the 'authority' the old man had spoken of at their first meeting, spoke to Boon Kong in his sleep and told him to leave the hermit's body outside the cave.

Quickly, he did as he was told. There was a clap of thunder, the likes of which Boon Kong had never heard before. It excited him and he watched eagerly for what would happen next. The sky turned black and through a gap in the clouds, a warrior-like figure on horseback appeared, surrounded by the brightest light he'd ever seen. It was so bright that it hurt his eyes to look at it, and he had to turn away.

A fierce wind howled around him, blowing him off his feet, and bowling him over into the cave. By the time he re-emerged, the sun was shining and there was no trace of the hermit, the wildcat or the raven.

Leaving the mountain, Boon Kong walked for days until he reached the provincial capital of Nan Wang. There, he found employment with a merchant who dealt in all types of precious metals and stones. Using a combination of his skills, he fashioned jewellery so fine that the local gentry almost came to blows in trying to buy. His skills soon trebled the merchant's wealth, and he too became very wealthy as a result.

In fact, he became so successful that the merchant became fearful of his own position and forced him to leave. This did not worry Boon Kong, for now he had enough contacts to run his own business trading in commodities, as well as producing the jewellery he had built his reputation on. He soon became the richest man in the whole province.

With his riches, he had a castle built in the mountains and secretly started to recruit his own army, remembering the hermit's advice about the copper armour. One evening, as he rode homeward to the castle flanked by his bodyguards, a large bright figure on horseback appeared on the path. Boon

Kong instantly recognised the rider as the God of the Clouds.

As he warily trotted toward the god, Boon Kong became aware that his guards and their horses had become motionless as if in a trance. "You are doing well," boomed the god. "I am very pleased and have given you six dragons to guard your castle. I shall contact you again nearer the time."

"Nearer what time?" wondered Boon Kong, but there was no answer. The horse reared up on its hind legs then silently galloped up into the sky. Instantly, the guards and their horses started moving again. They had no knowledge of what had taken place and were astonished when they arrived back at the castle to be greeted by the sight of the dragons.

Boon Kong told his men not to be afraid as the dragons were there to protect them. Smiling, he strode back into the castle. Everything was falling into place.

CHAPTER 7

26th August 2001

"Thanks John," said Tommy, opening and closing the penknife John had brought back for him. "That'll come in useful."

"It's not much," muttered John, "but there wasn't a huge choice." Looking around, John noticed that several items of furniture had been moved in the family's sitting room. "What's going on?" he asked Tommy.

"It's Gran's funeral on Wednesday and some relatives are coming up from London. I've got an aunt coming from San Francisco … in America."

"I know where San Francisco is!" retorted John.

"She's a famous lawyer there," Tommy said as Mrs Tan came into the room, dragging the vacuum cleaner in one hand, a feather duster in the other. Grumpily, she snapped something at Tommy in Chinese then turned the vacuum cleaner on, making further conversation impossible.

"We'd better move," said Tommy with a grin, making sure his mother didn't see it. "She's been going mad cleaning for the last two days."

"I'd better go," said John.

"Yeah, maybe," said Tommy. "I probably won't see you till after the funeral, but I'll look out for you on the way home from school on Thursday."

Sure enough, Tommy was waiting for John on Thursday afternoon. He looked much better than the last time John had seen him.

"So, how did it go?" John asked his friend.

"Well," said Tommy, "the funeral was sad, but Auntie Dotty cheered me up. She's brilliant, so funny, and knows all sorts of stories about famous people. I wish she could stay for a month!" Eyes sparkling, he continued breathlessly, "She makes me laugh so much, and Mai Ling follows her everywhere. Oh, and she wants to see your book too, as she's dead interested in the bowl and chopsticks. Do you have time to have tea with us now?"

John nodded, as he was curious to meet her. The boys had to catch a bus to get to the restaurant, which was in a part of town with which they were not familiar. John's jaw dropped and his eyes widened as he looked the building up and down.

"Are you sure this is right?" he asked Tommy.

"Yep, this is The Oasis—that's where she said."

As they opened the polished brass door, a man with a flower in his jacket lapel approached them. "Yes, gentlemen," he said, "may I be of assistance to you?"

John, who was struck dumb, wanted to leave, but Tommy instantly piped up, saying, "Yes please, we're meeting Miss Lim, could you show us to her table?"

"Ah yes, she is expecting you, come this way."

The man glided through the tables until they reached one tucked away in a corner, behind a huge potted palm which would have been more at home in the Botanical Gardens.

"Your guests, madam," he announced, then glided away. John felt even more uncomfortable when he saw Tommy's aunt, who didn't look like any aunt in John's family. Instead, she looked like a fashion model. From her shiny, beautifully styled hair, down to her pretty turquoise shoes, she was unlike anyone John had ever met. He could not stop staring, taking in every detail from her silk blouse to her beautiful jewelled and enamelled brooch.

"Hello boys, glad you could make it. You must be John." She offered John her hand and he blushed furiously, trying to smile as he briefly held the delicate fingers with their perfectly red-painted nails. "My name is Dorothy," she continued, "but my friends call me Dotty, mostly with good reason!"

She laughed easily, revealing a perfect set of beautiful white teeth. John found himself laughing too and felt slightly more at ease. Tommy was right—she was terrific.

"Well boys, first things first, let's get some tea shall we?" She held an immaculately manicured hand in the air for an instant and three waiters appeared as if by magic. The one who got there first stood poised with pad and pen at the ready. "I think we'll have the Traditional English Tea for three please, if that's all right with everybody?" She surveyed the party for dissenting looks, and seeing none, nodded to the waiter to indicate that he could leave.

"Now John, I understand you have an interest in antiques, in between demolishing people's houses!" John laughed, partly to release the tension he was still feeling and partly because of the casual way with which the observation was made. Diners at other tables turned to observe the odd trio and then returned to their meals, muttering.

As the meal progressed, John began to feel more comfortable. There was a fine view through huge windows onto the canal and several barges passed by while they were eating. Luckily, John had remembered to bring his book with him and was able to show Dotty the picture of the bowl and chopsticks, so that she would recognise it when she went through Tommy's gran's belongings.

When they had all finished, Dotty paid the bill, and Tommy and John thanked her for what had turned out to be a great time. But there was yet another surprise — jangling a set of keys, Dotty led the boys to a BMW parked round the corner, which she'd hired for the trip. She certainly knew how to drive it too!

By the time they arrived back at the Tans' house, both the boys' hearts were racing. John waved goodbye and went home, still buzzing after the hair-raising drive.

"And where d'yer think you've been, lad?" John's mother was not in any mood to hear about the English cream tea, the fancy restaurant, the fancy car, or even about glamorous Chinese aunts for that matter.

A plate, with what had been food a few hours before, was slammed down in front of John, and his mother stood with her hands on her hands on hips, daring him not to eat the smouldering ruins which had been his supper.

When Tommy and Mai Ling got back from school the next afternoon, they found Dotty in the sitting room. She had just asked Mr Tan to bring the trunks down from the loft so she could sort through her mother's possessions.

To Tommy's surprise, his dad seemed very reluctant to do as Dotty requested and complained about his back being too sore to do any heavy lifting. Dotty, smelling a rat, demanded the key to the padlock on the door and told them that she would fetch the things herself. This shamed Mr Tan into action and reluctantly, one by one, he carried the chests down into the old lady's bedroom.

Tommy eagerly lent Dotty a hand, while the rest of the family went downstairs to open the takeaway for business and prepare the evening meal for the family. Together, Tommy and Dotty spent a couple of hours sorting through the clothes, shoes, mementoes and general bric-a-brac of his gran's life.

There was, however, no sign of the bowl and chopsticks, or several of the other items, which Tommy had described. Dotty asked Tommy if he was sure he hadn't made up some of the descriptions, but he vehemently told her that both John and he had seen the things he'd told her about, in the chest.

"Right," said Dotty, "let's see who knows what, shall we?" She proceeded downstairs, followed by Tommy. Entering the kitchen, she asked Mr and Mrs Tan about the missing items. Tommy's parents looked extremely uncomfortable and tried to tell her that they had no idea what she was talking about.

Dotty's eyes narrowed. In her best courtroom manner, she informed the Tans that her mother had told her that several of the missing items were to have come to her when she died. She insisted that her mother would never have sold the items that had been brought over from China. Fixing the Tans with a stern look, she asked where the items were.

The parents wilted under this attack. Sighing, Mr Tan said, "All right, they were there. I admit it. As you can see, we haven't much money, so we took some of the nicest things to Manchester and sold them to help us pay for the funeral."

Dotty was silent for a moment, before quietly saying, "You could, and should, have asked me for some help. That's what families are for." She sighed, then stood up. "Can you remember the name of the shop you took them to?"

Luckily, Mr Tan had picked up a business card in the shop. Dotty decided to visit it first thing in the morning to see if they could get the items back. As it was Saturday, she invited Tommy and John along for the journey.

The next morning Tommy and Dotty were up with the lark. They tiptoed downstairs and out to the BMW. Dotty drove swiftly to the Cresswells' home, where she screeched to a halt in the cobbled gutter. Tommy leapt out and knocked on John's front door. Getting no answer, he lifted the letterbox and half shouted, half whispered John's name. Eventually, John came downstairs and opened the door, still far from awake.

"We're going into Manchester to try and get the bowl and chopsticks back," hissed Tommy.

"What? Why?" asked John.

"No time now, get dressed if you want to come, only hurry!" John, suddenly wide awake, threw himself back up the stairs, shouting that he was off to Manchester with Tommy to his bewildered father who had ventured out to see what the commotion was.

If there'd been a section in the Guinness Book of Records for speed dressing, John's name would have been in there. In record time, they were driving off, chatting excitedly.

None of them noticed a Mini, which was parked across the road, suddenly cough into life and follow them at a discreet distance. The driver had quite a job to keep up with the BMW and occasionally cursed, clenching his ferrety teeth in frustration.

Apart from some early-morning buses, there wasn't a great deal of traffic on the road, but Dotty's progress was delayed by endless sets of traffic lights. The tree-lined suburbs gave way to a more urban environment dotted with factories. Eventually, they found themselves driving through the heart of the city, then out again towards Cheetham Hill.

When they were almost at their destination, Dotty pulled in to check the map, unwittingly forcing Ferret-Teeth to come to a quick stop some way behind them so he wouldn't be spotted. After working out their route, she started driving again, taking several turns, until they found themselves in front of the shop.

Getting out of the car, they clustered in front of the shop, watched by Ferret-Teeth, who had parked behind another car so he wouldn't be seen. It was a rather run-down looking place, with things piled higgledy-piggledy in the window. The trio spent several minutes in animated conversation before getting back in the car and driving off again.

Quickly, Ferret-Teeth drove along the road until he too was opposite the shop. Very deliberately, he switched off the engine and sat there. He had waited a very long time for this moment and wanted to savour it.

Getting out of the car, he strolled casually over to the shop window. He saw what he was after almost immediately, but deliberately looked at other things, hardly believing that the objects were there, almost close enough to touch.

His eyes kept on returning to the bowl and chopsticks, half expecting them to vanish, but no, there they were, and at a ridiculously low price! The shopkeeper obviously had no clue as to their real worth.

Ferret-Teeth was itching to touch the objects, but the shop was dark and shuttered. The sign on the door read:

Opening Hours:
Mon to Fri 10am – 5pm
Sat 9am – 12am

Ferret-Teeth looked at his watch. It was ten past nine, but the shop was clearly closed. Puzzled, he glanced at the door again and spotted a small note in the corner which read:

Closed all day Saturday this week.

Open as usual on Monday.

What a stroke of luck! Congratulating himself on his good fortune, he strolled back to the car, with the closest thing to a smile he'd ever had on his lips.

Meanwhile, back in the BMW, Dotty was telling the boys about her plan to return to Manchester on Monday morning, and buy the bowl before heading down to London. "I'll phone on Monday evening to let you know that I've got the bowl," she promised.

Monday evening found Tommy pacing back and forth like a nervous cat, willing the phone to ring until his mother got annoyed and told him to help in the kitchen if he had nothing better to do.

At last the phone rang. Tommy jumped as if he'd touched a live wire. Dropping the dishcloth, he ran back to the phone and snatched it up, shouting, "Jade-Garden-Takeaway-good-evening-can-I-help-you!"

"Hello Tommy, is that you?"

"Yes, Auntie. Are you in London?"

"Yes, but I've got bad news. When I got to the shop this morning, the bowl, the chopsticks and the parchment were gone."

"Did you find out who'd bought them?"

"Nobody actually bought them. The owner said a man came in and asked about them, then when he turned round to check the price, the man grabbed the things and disappeared. From the description, it sounds like the chap you described from the bookshop!"

"But, how could Ferret-Teeth have known the things were there?"

"I don't know. Tommy, have a talk with John. I'm free on Thursday, so if you two can come down to London for the day, we'll try to think of a plan. I'll phone again on Wednesday evening. It's a shame that rat got there first."

"He's not a rat, he's a ferret," muttered Tommy, as he slumped against the wall.

Tommy had arranged to meet John the next day after school, but he was so upset about Ferret-Teeth that he slipped out and across the street to the Cresswells' home, to tell John there and then.

Mrs Cresswell answered the door and looked surprised to see Tommy. "Hello love," she said, "you'll be wanting John I s'pose?"

"Yes please. I'm sorry to bother you, but …"

"Never mind that, Tommy. Up you go. He's upstairs in his bedroom. You know the way." John was near the end of a game of Dungeons and Dragons and couldn't break off to talk to him straight away, so Tommy sat on the bed and read comics. After a few minutes he became impatient. "Haven't you finished, yet? I've got things to tell you," he said.

"In a minute, in a minute," said John as he pulled the joystick.

"Okay, if that's more important, I'll see you tomorrow," said Tommy. John pushed the controller away in disgust.

"All right, then," he groaned, "that would have been my best-ever score, so this had better be good." As Tommy blurted out what had happened, John looked at him with disbelief. He agreed that the mystery thief had to be Ferret-Teeth. From Dotty's description it couldn't have been anyone else.

"Well, there's only one thing for it, we'll have to go down to London on Thursday and see if your aunt will take us to Tidlington to try and get it back," he exclaimed.

"But he'll never sell it to us after all the trouble he's gone to get it."

"I know that!" said John. "So … maybe we have to get it back like he got it, by devious means!"

CHAPTER 8

Northern Provinces, Ancient China

18th March 648 AD

As Boon Kong's wealth and power increased, so did his need for recognition. By this time, he had built large barracks near his castle, as well as set up several copper mines in the surrounding mountains. He got poor youths from the surrounding villages to recruit their friends for his ever-growing army. He paid his soldiers well and provided each of them with armour he made from his special copper. By cleverly recruiting monks who were martial-arts experts to teach his troops, he built his army into a formidable force.

One evening, just as spring was awakening and the mountain streams were turning into swollen torrents from the melting winter snow, Boon Kong became aware of a presence in his library. It was the God of the Clouds. This time, there was no bright light, clap of thunder or lightning bolts. Boon Kong was surprised at how small the god, who had appeared so big and powerful on horseback, now looked.

"Good!" said the god observing Boon Kong's relaxed appearance. "You are fearless! The time has come for you to advance to Wat Su's Kingdom and take it for us."

Boon Kong smiled. "I am glad you consider me worthy to carry out this task," he said. "I shall not fail you."

"So be it!" said the god. "Proceed in your own way, in your own time, but make sure you have secured it by the time the crops are harvested." With that, he was gone.

Boon Kong immediately cleared a space on his table and rolled out a map of the kingdom, which he had specially prepared. Within days he had begun his campaign.

Because Wat Su had posted only a handful of his troops in the north of the Kingdom, Boon Kong found it easy to overrun them and take all the villages and towns in the locality. As his troops fanned out across the countryside, he decided to pursue some personal revenge and issued instructions for any pandas found to be caught and brought back to his castle to be put to work in the mines.

His men, realising that their master hated the pandas, took advantage of this fact and amused themselves by treating the helpless animals as cruelly as they could. The poor creatures were crammed into wooden cages and loaded onto wagons, which were pulled back to the mountains by teams of horses. They were provided with barely enough bamboo shoots to keep them alive. Many died on the journey, as the stress of the bad treatment and lack of food and water took their toll.

When the surviving pandas reached Boon Kong's mountain stronghold, a grim fate awaited them. Their cages were roughly dragged from the carts and thrown to the ground by the jeering men. They were then tied up and dragged inside the mine, which smelled so dreadful that it made newcomers retch as they entered. Large flickering torches set in recesses in the walls lit the gruesome scene.

The pandas were herded into treadmills, which were huge wooden wheels, attached to pumps. As the mines were constantly flooding from the mountain streams, the pandas were whipped day and night to keep them turning the wheels non-stop. The pandas were not alone. Any villagers captured in the raids were also put to work in the mines and often succumbed to illness. The villagers left standing were forced down narrow passages with only a small candle for light and made to hack away at the copper ore with only a crude pickaxe as a tool. When they weren't working, the pandas and humans alike were shackled in cages and given only the bare minimum of food and drink to keep them alive.

CHAPTER 9

Manchester, England

6ᵗʰ September 2001

On the evening before their trip, the two boys spent hours studying bus and train timetables in John's front room.

At one point Mr Cresswell popped his head round the door and looked at them curiously. "Are you off somewhere, then?" he asked them jokily. Both boys jumped and shot glances at each other. They knew that if they answered the question truthfully, Mr Cresswell would instantly forbid them to go. However, before either had a chance to open their mouths, he chuckled to himself and left them to it.

The boys sagged in relief and got back to their job.

"Why don't we get the quarter-past-six bus to the train station?" Tommy asked John, "then we could catch the ten past seven train to London." John thought about it for a moment and agreed.

"Hope the bus isn't late or we've had it," he added.

They made up their minds to tell no one about their plans apart from Dotty, who had arranged to meet the boys off the train at Euston station in London.

John and Tommy hardly slept a wink on Wednesday night, because apart from the journey itself, neither of them had been to London before. Both boys crept out of their homes like cat burglars at five-thirty on Thursday morning and met as planned in the main road opposite the park.

They were both so nervous that their bladders seemed to need emptying every few minutes and they had to take it in turns to rush over to use the toilets in the park, leaving the other to watch for the bus. There was hardly a soul around apart from some middle-aged cleaning ladies waiting at the bus stop. The sun peeped through the trees in the park.

At quarter past six, as John was crossing the road for the second time, Tommy spotted the bus coming. Hurriedly, John ran back, and the boys scrambled onboard.

As they waited for their journey to start, John suddenly froze and turned to Tommy with a look of real horror on his face. "Oh no!" he said, "I forgot to bring money for the train fare."

Tommy said nothing but produced a large green note from his blazer pocket and carefully unfolded it. It was a £50 note. "It's my savings," he explained. "My parents pay me when I help them in the takeaway."

"You're a little marvel!" said John, grabbing him round the neck in a bear hug, almost wrenching his head off his shoulders.

"That's enough!" said the conductor, who had wandered up the aisle. "Where are you lads going?"

"We're going to Manchester. To the train station. How

much is two half fares, please?"

"Forty pence each." Tommy offered him the £50 note. The conductor looked at the note and snorted, "Are you joking? Get off!" Luckily for the two boys, the old lady behind them interrupted.

"I'll give you change for the fifty," she snapped. "Now, conductor, please ring the bell to depart. I have a train to catch!"

The conductor, who knew he was beaten, meekly took the money and rang the bell. John was tempted to grab Tommy's neck again, but resisted the urge and instead mock-punched him in the ribs. Tommy responded by making Kung Fu moves back at John. They both started to laugh uncontrollably.

CHAPTER 10

Northern Provinces, Ancient China

10th July 650 AD

Nobody had ever seen how the copper from Boon Kong's mines had been used to make the armour for his soldiers, as he made it in a secret room deep in the castle. Although the armour was so thin that it hardly weighed anything, nothing could penetrate it. No knife, sword, lance, dagger or arrow had ever been known to pierce it.

The magical armour, the reason why Boon Kong's soldiers had become so invincible, was was why Wat Su and Chou Ping were meeting yet again. As they had many times before, the two men had gathered for a council-of-war with General Lu Shen in the Throne Room of the palace.

"How is this … this … peasant making my troops look like fools?" Wat Su demanded. "I need answers and I need them now. Not in a month's time, when it will be too late!"

"It is the armour, Excellency," said Lu Shen. "Boon Kong's troops are younger and less experienced than ours, but we cannot inflict serious injury on them, though they are able to damage our troops."

"I suggest a raid on his stronghold to disable his mines and armour-making facility," said Chou Ping.

"That's all very well, but what about the armour they are already wearing? We need to do something about that!" shouted Wat Su.

"Well, Excellency," said Chou Ping, "I think it must somehow be treated with a charm or spell. It is too thin to be so resistant on its own. If we could find out how he does it, we may be able to use our own magic to undo his."

"Let's ask him next time he pops in to say hello, shall we?" bellowed Wat Su, kicking over a plant stand. He had become more and more desperate as he heard news of the enemy's advance, along with the news of the imminent extinction of the pandas.

"Master, all is not lost," said Chou Ping. "I believe we have a good solution to try."

"Go on," said Wat Su, sitting down at a small table, his face buried in his hands. Chou Ping took a deep breath. He knew what he was about to say would not go down well, but decided it was his duty to suggest it.

"Desperate times call for desperate measures. Isn't that right?" he asked the other two. "I think it is time to ask Monkey for help."

Both Wat Su and Lu Shen groaned.

"Are you serious?" demanded Lu Shen. "Monkey always creates more problems than he solves, and *never* takes anything seriously!"

Wat Su, however, was reluctantly nodding his agreement. "Send word that we request his presence," he growled.

Monkey was a god who lived in Heaven, but often came

down to Earth as he enjoyed meddling in the affairs of men more than most. His presence generally caused havoc.

Sure enough, he arrived in his usual fashion, upsetting the ladies in the Palace by suddenly appearing when they were bathing. After satisfying himself that they had shrieked themselves hoarse, he grinned, bowed to them and flew off to join the men.

Monkey was told of the problems as soon as he arrived. Wasting no time, he leapt straight into action and flew to the north of the Kingdom with his Magic Staff to see if he could attack Boon Kong in his stronghold. But he found that the dragons guarding the sorcerer and his castle were too dangerous. He had to return to Wat Su's kingdom once more.

CHAPTER 11

Manchester, England

7th September 2001

Tommy and John ran onto the station, bought their tickets, and made it onto the train before the doors closed. They collapsed into their seats, surrounded by businessmen reading newspapers. One regarded them with a frown, before leaning over to say, "Do you know this is a first-class carriage? If you don't have the right ticket you'll have to pay the difference when the inspector comes round."

John was taken aback, but thanked the man for pointing that out. Keeping an eye out for the train conductor, they moved down the lurching train to search for the standard class compartments, but every carriage was full. Why were all these people going to London, and so early in the morning? Eventually they found two seats together, much further down the train.

As they moved closer to London, each stop brought more travellers. After what seemed like an eternity, the fields and canals gave way to houses, factories and high brick embankment walls still thick with soot, even though it had been many times the boys' lifetimes since steam trains ran between them.

Euston station was big, but Dotty, mindful of the fact that the boys hadn't done any travelling on their own, made sure she was at the ticket barrier to meet them. They all smiled thankfully when they met, glad to see each other again.

"Well," said Dotty, "have you eaten yet?"

"We had some crisps and chocolate on the train," said Tommy.

"And some tea too," said John.

"Tea too, eh?" mimicked Dotty, making them all laugh. "Look boys," she said as they walked to the car, "I've checked the map, and if we leave now we can get down to Tidlington by late afternoon. So, let's go!"

Dotty eased the powerful car into the late-morning traffic, which thankfully wasn't very heavy. The route she chose didn't pass any of London's better-known landmarks, but from the A40M they could see the Post Office Tower, which was better than nothing. The roads were all quite wide, and the traffic flowed freely.

Before too long, they connected with the motorway to Devon and Dotty took full advantage of the car's performance to try and get there in the least possible time.

"Let's get this show on the road!" she laughed as she roared off.

Before long, they ground to a halt, because of an accident several miles ahead. But after crawling along for what seemed like an age, everything started to pick up speed again and soon they were whizzing along once more. After a few hours, they realised that they were going to arrive later than they had originally planned, and that the bookshop would be closed when they got there, but they kept their fingers crossed that Ferret-Teeth lived above it as they didn't have a clue where to start looking for him, other than the shop.

Dotty drove as fast as she dared and before long they saw the rather neglected-looking signpost, pointing left, with the name of their destination marked on it.

Dusk was just starting to fall as they drove slowly through the village, eyes straining as they passed the bookshop. The sign said CLOSED, but they could make out a light shining through the bead curtain at the back of the shop.

"Right," said John, "let's park in the pub car park, right up the back where it's dark. Ferret-Teeth has probably seen this car, so we'd better keep it out of sight. You two stay here, and I'll go and have a look round. I know this place better than you."

"But what are you going to do?" asked Tommy, the tension in his voice quite audible.

"I won't know till I get there!" said John, trying to mask his nerves with bravado.

Dotty spoke softly, "Listen John, for your own good, and mine, don't do anything which is against the law. Or if you do, don't tell me about it!"

Tommy thought about the situation. "It won't be illegal if we get the stuff back," he mused. "After all, Ferret-Teeth stole the bowl, and we're just going to get it back so we can buy it off the man in the shop. Wait up, John, I'm coming with you."

John could feel his heart thumping and there was a strange

sensation at the bottom of his stomach as they crossed to the other side of the street. Carefully, they studied the building, looking for possible escape routes. A thick creeper ran all over the top of the shops, between the signs and the windows. It certainly looked strong enough to provide support if they had to leave that way. Making sure nobody could see them, they crossed back again and slipped quietly along the side of the building. They passed the back of the newsagents, which was closed and totally deserted, and crept on.

On the wall at the back of the bookshop, there was a door and one window. A light was on in the room, but the curtains weren't drawn. John flattened himself to the wall and indicated to Tommy to do the same. Very slowly, very quietly, they slid right next to the window. Ever so gently John moved his head round the edge, so he could see inside. The sash window was slightly open.

The room seemed to be empty. There was a table, which had the lamp on it, two chairs, a couple of armchairs, and a sideboard bearing various ornaments and a few bottles of alcohol. Ducking under the window, just in case Ferret-Teeth came in while they were passing it, they moved down to the back door.

Grasping the handle with both hands, John turned it. It made a slight noise, so he stopped and waited, his hands slippery with fear. After a few minutes of silence, he slowly tried turning it again, this time managing to twist it all the way around. Gently, he pushed against the door. Nothing happened. It was locked.

He looked at Tommy. "You're smaller than me," he whispered. "We can't get in the door. If we push the window up, do you think you can get in?"

"Of course."

They moved back down the wall to the window once more and inserted their fingers under the bottom of the window sash. It was very tight, but they managed. Gently they pushed it up far enough for Tommy to squeeze through.

Once in the room Tommy quickly scanned it for the bowl, but there was no sign of it. He quietly crossed the room to the door and went into the passage. Opposite him was a staircase that led upstairs. To his left, the passageway led to a recess, where Tommy knew the back door would be. Quickly he went to the door, and finding the key in the lock, he turned it, in case he needed to get out that way. He came back up the passage, past the room and staircase, to the other end, where he saw the beaded curtain at the back of the shop. He peeped through into the shop, but there was no sign of life, so he went back into the sitting room again.

Unsure of where to start, Tommy decided to search the sideboard first. He was about to open its door, when he heard voices. A thousand thoughts raced through his head. What if they caught him? How could he explain being there? What would happen to John, and Dotty? The voices got louder. Tommy heard Ferret-Teeth's voice saying, "Yes, the silly little devils led me straight to it, couldn't have been better if I'd planned it, they'll have no idea where it is."

Tommy realised that he couldn't leave the room. Quickly he raised the tablecloth and vanished underneath it, just as the two men entered.

The second man was talking now, and from his accent, Tommy guessed he was Chinese. "If indeed you have got what you say, it is a miracle. These bowls are very rare. The emperors had most of them destroyed when they were trying to break the power of the sorcerers. Only a handful survived," he said.

"We've got not only the bowl, not only the chopsticks, but the parchment too!" said Ferret-Teeth. The other man could hardly contain his excitement.

"You mean …"

"Yes," interrupted Ferret-Teeth, "we can do what nobody has been able to do for centuries. We can travel through time!"

CHAPTER 12

Prince Wat Su's Palace, Southern Provinces, Ancient China

12th July 650 AD

Monkey wasn't happy. His journey to the north had proved fruitless and he was becoming exasperated. He paced up and down the Throne Room, tapping the floor with his staff as he went. Chou Ping and the others watched him nervously, as he was famed for his unpredictability. As he paced, the faces of inquisitive soldiers could be seen peering down through the narrow windows above. All of a sudden, Monkey rose in the air, and, talking to himself, proceeded to move over to one of the windows and pulled faces at the men on the other side.

"What is he doing now?" groaned Lu Shen, taking off his helmet and rotating his head to ease his aching neck.

"He is probably considering the best course of action," replied Chou Ping, lamely. As suddenly as he had risen, Monkey leapt down next to them again.

"Yes," he said, "Chou Ping is right. I have been thinking hard about matters." He beckoned Chou Ping to join him out of earshot of the others. "I believe," Monkey began, "that we need to do something really unexpected."

"Such as?" hissed Chou Ping.

"I believe we need to ask our future beings for help."

"I don't understand a single word you are saying!" fumed Chou Ping.

"We," said Monkey, "need to get Prince Wat Su's descendant to come back from the future to help us."

"How exactly do we do that then?" queried Chou Ping.

"Listen closely ..." said Monkey with a grin.

CHAPTER 13

Devon, England

7th September 2001

Tommy had become increasingly uncomfortable trapped under the table. Being very careful not to make a sudden move, he looked about him and noticed that the light on the table was plugged into an adapter that was sticking out from socket right next to him. This gave him the beginnings of a plan on how to escape.

But, as he stretched out his hand, the two men moved to the table. Tommy heard several items being placed on the surface above his head. He crossed his fingers and prayed that they were the items he had been searching for.

"Over there, on the sideboard," said Ferret-Teeth to the other man, "I've got another copy of the book I gave the boy." Picking up their drinks, they moved across the room.

Taking a deep breath, Tommy peered around the edge of the tablecloth and saw the two men studying the book on the sideboard. He took several more deep breaths and made a mental note of where the door, window and men were. In one swift motion he pulled the plug and adapter out of the socket, plunging the room into darkness.

The two men cried out in surprise. The room was not as dark as he'd hoped, but there was nothing Tommy could do. Quietly, he came out from under the table and pulled the adapter from the plug, then threw the adapter at the window as hard as he could. The glass shattered with a spectacular noise, causing John, waiting on the other side, to dive for cover, and several dogs to start barking. Quickly, Tommy felt for the objects on the table. Yes! He had found the parchment, bowl and chopsticks! Picking them up, he slid the chopsticks into his jacket's inside pocket and forced the bowl into the outside pocket. The parchment, he put as gently as he could into his other pocket.

The two men meanwhile, thinking that someone had thrown a brick at them through the window, were crouching down on the floor. When they heard the door open, they cowered more, expecting someone to come in, not go out.

It was only when they heard the back door open, and Tommy and John's footsteps running past the window, that they realised what had happened.

"Quick, after them!" snarled Ferret-Teeth, switching on the main room light. "They've got the bowl!"

Tommy and John ran into the car park at full tilt. Luckily, Dotty heard the noise and was ready to go. As soon as they appeared, the engine started, the lights came on, and the car moved forward to meet them. Opening the doors, the boys threw themselves in, with Tommy shouting, "Quick, get going, auntie — they're coming!"

Dotty accelerated away. The headlights revealed the two men just entering the car park, but Dotty didn't hesitate. She drove straight at them, causing them to dive out of the way, showering them with gravel as she slewed out onto the road.

"Did you get the stuff?" asked Dotty, excitedly.

"Yes," said John, "but how long they'll let us keep them, I don't know!"

"Perhaps Auntie can take them out the country," said Tommy. Dotty gave no reply. She was driving as fast as she dared, knowing that the two men would probably not be far behind.

When they got to Exeter, Dotty told the boys that it would be best if they stopped there for the night, as she was very tired. She drove around for a good half an hour to make sure that there was no sign of their pursuers, before pulling into a quiet side street where she'd noticed a sign for a bed-and-breakfast.

John and Tommy phoned home, to let their parents know that everything was all right, while Dotty asked Mrs O'Rourke, the landlady, to prepare two rooms.

From Tommy's face it was clear that his mother was not happy about the situation. She asked to speak to Dotty, and the boys heard her shouting from where they were standing. Mrs Tan was obviously getting her own back for being told off for selling the family heirlooms.

Dotty stood there and listened with a look of resignation on her face, and when she managed to get a word in, made Mrs Tan promise to tell Mrs Cresswell that the boys were quite safe. Everybody was tired and hungry, so they bought some lamb kebabs in a nearby takeaway and joined Dotty in her room to plan their next move.

While Dotty pulled three chairs up to the table in the corner of her room, Tommy got out the bowl and set it gently down on the table. It was the first time any of them had had a chance to see it at close quarters in a good light. It was beautiful. The porcelain itself was extremely delicate and the pale colours were pleasing to the eye. They studied it as they ate.

Dotty, having finished her food and carefully wiped her fingers, was just about to pick up the bowl to examine it, when they heard a noise at the window.

"What was that?" asked Tommy, nervously.

"Probably just the wind, or maybe it's started raining," said John. Dotty went over to the window and pulled the curtain aside.

"Look, there's noth …" her voice trailed off and the colour drained from her face. She tried to pull the curtain back across again, but it was too late. They'd all seen the strange transparent disembodied mask floating there briefly before vanishing.

"Ferret-Teeth!" hissed John.

"Oh my goodness," said Dotty, losing her composure. She collapsed on the bed, ashen-faced.

"What was that … that thing?" asked John.

Dotty took a deep breath. "I'm not sure, but I think that was something called a 'hound'. It's said to be possible to split off a little part of yourself and send it to a different place, using dark magic. I've heard about hounds from my great-grandmother, but I'd always thought it was superstitious nonsense before."

"So, it's a sort of spirit?" volunteered Tommy.

"Yes, exactly," agreed his aunt. "If that thing really was a hound, Ferret-Teeth is far more dangerous than I'd thought. A hound is sent out to find something or someone the person wants. They say that to produce a hound drains you of energy for two or three days, because the amount of concentration required is unbelievable. The problem is that Ferret-Teeth knows exactly where we are now."

"We'd better go to the police," said John.

"And tell them what?" asked Tommy. "That we're being chased by an angry magician, who wants his bowl back? A bowl, which, by the way, we stole from him! They'd probably lock *us* up!"

"What else can we do, give it back?" said John.

"I doubt if that would be enough," said Dotty, "I don't want to frighten you, but I think we're in serious danger. We know too much about Ferret-Teeth now for our own good."

"Could we come to America with you?" asked Tommy.

Dotty shook her head and said, "Ferret-Teeth may have friends over there too. You know you were right Tommy, when you once called him a devil."

"What can we do then?" said John, who was starting to feel very scared indeed. What had started off as something of an adventure was turning into a nightmare.

"I think," said Dotty, "there's only one thing we can do."

CHAPTER 14

Prince Wat Su's Palace, Southern Provinces, Ancient China

12th July 650 AD

Monkey flung his arm across Chou Ping's shoulder and started walking. "I can summon the Prince's descendant myself, from the future," he boasted.

He smiled encouragingly at Chou Ping as they joined the others.

"Well?" demanded Wat Su.

"I think we may have the answer to our troubles, Excellency," Chou Ping said, ignoring Lu Shen's hostile gaze. "Monkey is going to perform a very difficult feat, which will require all of us not to interrupt him in any way, and do whatever he tells us." The prince shot a look at Monkey, who was standing by the small table, with eyes closed, murmuring to himself. Wat Su's patience snapped.

"What is this mumbo-jumbo?" he demanded. "I ask for action, and all I get is a muttering monkey!" He moved as if to strike Monkey, but Chou Ping placed himself in the way.

"Please Master, patience," he said. "Monkey is trying

something which needs all his concentration. If he loses it, it could cause us or them to vanish into the third time zone."

"And who is this 'them' you mention?" demanded Wat Su.

"All in good time, Excellency, you soon will see," Chou Ping reassured him.

CHAPTER 15

Exeter, England

7th September 2001

"You mean … use the bowl?" asked John, grimly.

"Yes," said Dotty. "If that book was right and it can allow us to time travel, that will give us enough breathing space to escape from Ferret-Teeth."

Dotty sat on the bed, alternately studying the parchment then John's book, and another book about Chinese magic she'd bought in London. For what seemed like ages, she sat there mouthing words, and occasionally cross-checking something in one of the books.

Eventually John could stand it no longer and said, "Ferret-Teeth must be very close by now!"

Dotty said nothing, but glanced up at him with a look that made him wish he'd kept silent. At last she said, "I think that's all I need to know. Listen very carefully to what I'm going to tell you. I'm not exaggerating when I say your lives will depend on it." She told them that once she had started the spell, on no account whatsoever were they to make a move.

Moving purposefully to the table, Dotty put the bowl in the middle. She then placed the two chopsticks, one either side of the bowl with their tips touching behind the bowl, like an inverted 'V'.

Next she made John and Tommy stand facing the table, Tommy on the left, and John on the right. She took John's right hand and placed the index finger firmly on the end of the right hand chopstick. She then took John's left hand, and Tommy's right hand, and joined them together.

Moving to Tommy's left, she took his hand and placed the index finger on the end of the left hand chopstick. Finally, she checked that the tips of the chopsticks were still touching.

In effect, she had created a circle, using the two boys and the chopsticks, with the bowl in the middle. She took several deep breaths, and told them to do the same. Now sitting behind them, Dotty started to recite the words of the incantation, in a low, monotonous voice. This only went on for a couple of minutes or so, but seemed ten times that long to the boys. John started to think that the whole thing was a waste of time. How daft they must look, standing there holding hands!

He was near the point of exploding into a giggling fit, when he felt a strange sort of tingling sensation where his index finger touched the chopstick. Tommy had obviously felt it too, because he gave a little gasp and his fingers tightened on John's hand.

The feeling started to spread, slowly into their hands, and up into their arms. It was a bit like pins and needles. Dotty's intonation started to take on a new urgency.

At that moment, John, who had been looking ahead, glanced down at his hand and was horrified to see his finger slowly starting to de-materialise. It became almost transparent, and then sort of liquid, seeming to flow into the chopstick. Even as he watched, this phenomenon spread slowly up his arm. His head reeled with the sound of Dotty's voice, now accompanied by a strange rushing noise.

Dotty watched, fascinated, as both the boys flowed down into the chopsticks. When they had both completely disappeared, she got up and went over to the table.

As she watched, the tips of the chopsticks glowed slightly, and then a stream of luminous material slowly flowed across the table and up into the bowl.

Satisfied that the first part of the operation had been a success, she turned her attention to getting herself into the bowl. The spell she had to use this time was slightly different to the first one, as she had to ensure that the chopsticks and the parchment came along with her.

When she was sure that she had memorised the right words, she tucked the parchment into her belt. She then placed her right index finger on the right hand chopstick, and her left likewise.

She started to recite the words. As she did so, she became aware of voices from the hall downstairs. From the fragments of conversation she could make out, Dotty realised that Ferret-Teeth had arrived and was trying to convince the landlady that the Chinese friend who accompanied him was Tommy's uncle, and they wanted to surprise him.

Dotty realised that she only had a few seconds before they appeared, and speeded up her incantation accordingly. Soon, she experienced the same tingling sensation the boys had earlier, and watched herself slowly change into a different form. After about a minute, there was just an empty room, with a bowl and two chopsticks on the table.

Meanwhile, downstairs, a £20 note had induced a rapid change of heart in the landlady, and two pairs of footsteps rang on the staircase walls. Ferret-Teeth flung open the door, but alas, he was met by the sight of an empty room. Out of the corner of his eye, he spotted the bowl on the far table, which was just starting to de-materialise. With an animal-like cry, he sprang across the room, making a desperate lunge at the disappearing bowl. His fingers went straight through it as it vanished from sight.

CHAPTER 16

Prince Wat Su's Palace, Ancient China

7th September 650 AD

Wat Su's temper had begun to boil again, when a small movement on the tabletop caught his eye. As he watched, a bowl materialised in front of them, filled with a shiny transparent mist.

Slowly, the mist rose, and flowed over the edge of the bowl. Before long, they were able to see the shape of two chopsticks. The mist continued to form, now starting to flow from the end of the chopsticks. It rose across the table, and trickled down to the floor. Before their eyes, two very frightened boys appeared.

One was Chinese, but the other … Well, what a strange sight he was! Hair the colour of straw, eyes the colour of the sky, and such pale skin. Was he a god?

Before the men could say anything, the mist in the bowl started to move again, flowing down into the chopsticks. They all watched as it rose again from the far ends, rising up into the air before falling onto the floor. After about a minute a woman wearing strange clothes slowly materialised.

Some courtiers who had drifted into the Throne Room let out startled cries as they watched what was happening. "Get them out of here!" yelled Chou Ping, and summoned the guards to remove everybody, except the four of them.

The woman blinked, moved her fingers away from the ends of the chopsticks, and felt for the parchment tucked in her belt. She looked around in astonishment, only to see the others in the room looking at her in the same way.

Speaking in Mandarin, she asked the men where she was, but they couldn't understand her, because the language had changed over the years. Luckily, Monkey, who had come out of his trance-like state, was able to translate and told her that she was in the palace of his Imperial Majesty Prince Wat Su.

"Where did he say we are, Auntie?" asked Tommy, nervously.

"In Prince Wat Su's palace," she told him, "and that's all I know at the moment, but he says we are welcome, so don't be frightened."

Meanwhile, John was gazing in amazement at Monkey. "That's the monkey in my dream!" he whispered to Tommy.

Monkey turned to him and grinned. "Ah, you recognise me," he said, in perfect English. "I'm happy to meet you at last."

While Chou Ping was explaining what had happened to Wat Su and Lu Shen, Monkey told the three newcomers how he'd arranged for them to come back in time.

"So you *made* me go into the bookshop?" asked John.

"Yes," said Monkey, "because, without that book you

wouldn't have known why the bowl was so special. I had to guide you back to find it." John remembered the slight shiver he'd felt, as he pulled the book from the shelf.

"So, if I am Wat Su's relative does this mean I'm a prince, too?" asked Tommy.

Monkey laughed. "Well, not quite, because there are so many descendants between you and Wat Su, and you can't all be princes," said Monkey, giggling at the boy's downcast face.

"And where do I fit into all this?" asked Dotty.

"Ah, Most Beautiful One, without you to translate the manuscript, the boys would never have got here."

"I see ..." said Dotty thoughtfully.

All the while, the three newcomers had been looking around in awe. The Throne Room was big, reminding Dotty of the interior of a cathedral, though on a smaller scale. The boys gazed at the guards, with their tunics and helmets, who stood to attention as Wat Su strode over beaming, and bade them welcome with Monkey acting as interpreter.

The travellers were all shown into a large room next door, where a table had been loaded with all sorts of strange dishes. They needed no prompting to sit down and feast on the delicacies that their host had provided.

As they tucked into their meal of spicy meat dishes and plates of steaming vegetables, accompanied by a variety of hot sauces, Dotty suddenly felt a tugging sensation at her waist. She looked down, and to her horror, saw that the parchment, which she'd tucked into her belt, had developed a life of its own and was struggling to free itself.

She stood up, knocking over her chair. Everyone looked at her with alarm. The parchment finally freed itself and floated quickly through the air into the Throne Room next door. Everyone ran after it, and watched as it settled down onto the bowl, which was still on the table. Without warning, the parchment and chopsticks began to de-materialise.

John rushed to grab them but was held back by Monkey, who said, "No, don't touch it. It could kill you! Somebody's taking it back again." All three time-travellers had a good idea who that someone was.

"Oh no!" said Tommy, "it must be Ferret-Teeth. But will he be able to follow us here?"

"Don't worry," said Monkey, "if any enemy forces turn up here, they'll see how powerful our magic is."

Slowly and silently, they returned to the table to finish their meal, before being shown to their sleeping quarters.

Dotty had a huge room to herself, with several giggling maids to look after her. The boys had a smaller room, with two very low beds. Fierce-looking guards were posted outside their doors and the balconies outside the windows, to protect them. Normally this would have had the boys chattering nineteen to a dozen with excitement, but the disappearance of the parchment had put them in a serious mood.

"John," whispered Tommy. "How are we ever going to get back home?"

CHAPTER 17

Prince Wat Su's Palace, Ancient China

8th September 650 AD

The next morning, the boys were woken by Dotty who was dressed in a pale yellow silk robe embroidered with flowers and two large dragons. Her long hair was gathered on top of her head, and decorated with flowers.

"This wasn't my idea!" she said, as the boys looked at her in astonishment. "But I figured that I'd better go along with their wishes for the time being."

The boys found that the clothes they had left on the chairs had been replaced with dark blue silk tunics, laced sandals and close-fitting silk caps which came down to their ears. As they were the only clothes they could see, they had no choice but to wear them.

Tommy collapsed with laughter when he saw John dressed in his outfit, but John had to admit that Tommy really looked the part in his, and that maybe there was some royal blood in him, after all.

When they were all ready, servants led the trio down a

wide flight of stairs flanked by guards with fearsome-looking swords and daggers tucked into large leather sword belts, and then into a room where a huge table had been laid with breakfast.

Several other men who were already seated at the table rose to greet them as they entered.

The travellers caused quite a stir —John's face and hair were touched by several men, who obviously didn't believe he was real! Monkey called the council of war to order and introduced everyone.

The men round the table were either governors of the various provinces in the Kingdom, or commanders of the Prince's army. Over the last few months they had lost all hope of victory as they watched Boon Kong going from strength to strength. So pessimistic were they that they had been in the middle of making evacuation plans for the northern provinces when the boys had entered.

After the novelty of the travellers' arrival had died down, the men went back to their heated discussion, with several of them standing to shout and pound the table, making the crockery jump in the air.

"Please, gentlemen, please," shouted Chou Ping, struggling to make himself heard above the din. "Our new friends, who have travelled here from the future, are here to help us rid the kingdom of Boon Kong."

Questions such as, How are we going to help? and, Who is Boon Kong? bubbled from Tommy as Monkey translated for the benefit of the newcomers.

"All in good time, all in good time," said Monkey.

Dotty, who had been listening carefully, found she was

starting to understand the language a little more, and was able to take over the translating when Monkey was called on by the generals to explain the plan of action.

Picking up his staff, Monkey went over to the wall, on which a large map of the Kingdom had been pinned.

Monkey pointed out where Boon Kong's castle was and how much territory he'd gained. To Tommy's horror, he saw that Boon Kong was now in control of almost half the Kingdom!

"My plan is straightforward," Monkey said. "With my magic I can give the power of flight—for one full day from sunrise to sunset—to these three people when the moon is at its smallest. We will attack Boon Kong then." He smiled at Dotty and the others. "You call it the 'new moon'," he said for their benefit.

"What's going on?" hissed John, when Dotty had translated Monkey's speech.

"I don't know," said Dotty, trying not to look worried. She was good at masking her feelings, for her court appearances. "I'm sure Monkey will explain in a second."

However, Monkey had moved on and said nothing more about that subject. Instead, he pulled forward a scared-looking girl.

"This is Ching Lai," he announced. "She managed to escape from Boon Kong's castle last week and sought out our soldiers. We have smuggled her down here so that she can tell us about the castle and anything else which may be of use to us."

Ching Lai was very nervous, as she was not used to addressing people. She stood there silently, twisting her clothing and looking imploringly at Monkey. "It's all right, my dear," he told her reassuringly. "Just take your time and tell us as much as you can in your own words."

"I was kidnapped a few years ago from my village, which is more than a day away from the castle," she said. "They took me to the mine, which is just over a small rise near the castle. There, they are cruel to everyone and they whip the pandas." Overcome with bad memories, she started to sob.

"Take your time."

"Well," she continued, "the mine has many tunnels that run off in all directions. I think some lead underground back into the castle as none of the copper is ever brought back through the entrance, but somehow is taken back to the castle to be made into armour by Boon Kong.

"The castle itself is really hard to get into. It is guarded by dragons and the walls are too hard to climb. The only chance of gaining entry is if you go in from the battlements or turrets where the dragons can't reach … If you can get up there, that is. Monkey asked me to draw a rough plan of the inside of the castle. It shows where I think the armour-making room is."

Monkey took the plan from Ching Lai and gave it to the three visitors.

"Memorise it well," he told them gravely.

"Wait, you mean we have to go there?" Tommy asked nervously. Monkey looked at them, and nodded.

"The new moon is tomorrow," he said quietly. Stepping forward, Dotty protested.

"This is ridiculous, we're totally unprepared—and there just isn't enough time!"

"It has to be tomorrow," said Monkey, quietly. "Ching Lai

has told us something that makes it vital that we act right away. She says there are now only ten pandas left. These are the last ten to exist in the whole of China. All the rest have been killed off, or have died from disease or hunger. The chances are that those ten too will not last if we wait for the next new moon."

He went on to explain why the pandas were important to the gods and could not be allowed to die out.

"Well," said Dotty, "it seems we have no choice, then."

CHAPTER 18

Prince Wat Su's Palace, Southern Provinces, Ancient China

9th September 650 AD

Monkey suggested to Chou Ping that the commanders and governors should work out a plan of invasion and draw up detailed orders for their troops, which Monkey and the visitors could distribute to the field commanders they encountered as they flew up to the castle. Servants were summoned to clear away all the breakfast dishes, and the soldiers and Governors got to work forming a plan of action.

Meanwhile, Monkey and Chou Ping had strolled away from the others. "Do you suppose that the one they called Ferret-Teeth will follow our young friends here, as they fear?" Chou Ping asked Monkey.

"It's hard to say," replied Monkey, "but it's possible that he is working with Boon Kong."

"Yes," replied Chou Ping, thoughtfully stroking his wispy beard. "And if he is, Boon Kong may decide to bring him back to help, in the same way we brought Tommy and the others back."

Dotty, who had drifted close enough to eavesdrop, understood enough of the conversation to realise that Monkey thought there was a chance that Ferret-Teeth and his friend might transport themselves to Boon Kong's castle. If that happened, Monkey feared that their added powers might prove too much for him. With her heart pounding, Dotty decided to say nothing, as the boys were worried enough already without having that to think about as well.

After a few minutes, Monkey strode back over to the travellers and beckoned them to follow him to the Throne Room. As soon as they entered, Monkey flew up into the rafters, swooped down low past their astonished faces, then up once more, all the while shouting instructions to them about the positions they should adopt whilst flying the next day. He explained that it was not possible to give them the power until daybreak the next day, but that he needed to tell them how to fly now so as not to waste time the following morning.

"I've always wanted to learn to fly!" said Dotty enthusiastically, marvelling as they watched Monkey take off and glide effortlessly around the room. Secretly, all three wished that they didn't have to wait till the next morning to try for themselves.

They spent the rest of the morning learning about the postures they would need to adopt while in the air, and practised crouching with arms outstretched behind them or leaning backwards with knees slightly bent, which was the landing position.

After lunch, they studied Ching Lai's plans of the castle, spending an hour questioning her about everything they weren't sure of.

When they were no longer capable of taking in any more information, they were taken by Monkey and Chou Ping down a dank spiral staircase, which was poorly lit by guttering torches, to the Palace armoury. One of the large guards at the bottom of the stairs spent several laborious minutes unlocking the huge, thick reinforced copper door for them.

They lit several torches once inside and looked around in astonishment. The room was about twenty foot square. Secured against two of the walls were all manner of weapons, ranging from nine-ring broadswords, snake spears and long-handled axes, to bows and arrows, tiger forks and small daggers. Monkey invited them to choose their weapons for the following day.

"How on earth do you expect us to walk with any of those things, let alone fly?" Dotty asked him incredulously.

"Maybe you should choose a dagger, then," said Monkey quietly. They were also each given a set of the special light copper armour, which had been captured from Boon Kong's soldiers. Dotty marvelled at it, as it weighed next to nothing.

One of the guards helped them to try the armour on, talking excitedly all the while. "What's he saying?" Tommy asked.

"He's telling you how they got the armour," replied Monkey. "Apparently this chap and some others were on patrol when they came upon some of Boon Kong's men fast asleep round a fire. They were able to capture them and take them prisoner, which is how they got the armour."

After Monkey was sure that they were all happy with their weapons, he asked one of the commanders to give them a lesson in the use of daggers. Although he knew that they could not become experts in such a short time, Monkey hoped that the lesson would give them the edge they needed if their lives were put in danger the following day.

Although he couldn't speak English, the commander patiently demonstrated the best way to use the daggers, showing them how to circle and make quick lunging and feinting movements at the enemy. He pointed out where the weakest areas would be and made them practise with each other.

By the time the lesson was over, they were all very tired and hungry, so when Monkey called it a day, Dotty and the boys were relieved. "Go and get ready," he told them, "Prince Wat Su is giving a banquet in your honour."

After a rest and a good soak in the bath, the travellers felt revived. They went downstairs chatting happily and were shown to the banqueting hall where Prince Wat Su was waiting with his advisers and staff. As the visitors entered, a large shout went up and everybody rose to greet them.

When they were finally seated next to the prince, having managed to get through the forest of backslapping hands, wine-laced breath and well-meaning grins, the feasting started. Huge trays of crispy roast suckling pig appeared. Then gigantic plates of beef and bean curd were carried to the groaning tables, along with platters of steaming hot vegetables, a lot of which looked very unusual to the visitors. Before they'd had the chance to attack these dishes properly, the servants brought out vast tureens of soup from which came the most fabulous smells. Nobody needed any bidding to fill and refill their bowls, and everyone set to eagerly emptying the platters as fast as they appeared.

During the course of the magnificent banquet, several of the commanders came over, smiling and bowing, to offer their best wishes for the vital day ahead. Monkey also came over to engage them in conversation. However, he not only talked to them, he also secretly shook a few drops of liquid from a small phial he had concealed in his paw, into each of their drinks.

That done, he proposed a toast, to make sure they all drained their glasses. He smiled to himself, knowing that the potion he had given them would make them sleep soundly and give them plenty of energy for the challenging day ahead.

The next morning, as the grey sky began to show a hint of red on the horizon, Monkey woke everyone and gave them all a strange tasting, greenish-yellow fruit which had a spiky skin which they had to peel off.

"Eat up. We won't get a chance to eat again today, but this special fruit will give us strength for as long as we need it," said Monkey.

Afterwards, they put on their armour and made sure they had their daggers, before proceeding down the stairs to the banqueting room for a final briefing from Prince Wat Su.

"My loyal commanders, soldiers, trusted advisers, and honoured visitors. It is vital for the future of the country and our whole way of life that you go out and win today. All eyes will be on us, including several very important ones in the heavens. I will not waste any more time except to say good luck to you all, especially those who have the hazardous mission of penetrating the castle!"

He called on a soldier who had arrived during the night to give the latest positions of Boon Kong's troops, and started issuing his orders to the commanders present. Monkey, meanwhile, had collected the written orders for the field commanders, which they were to distribute on their way to the Boon Kong's castle. As soon as he was done, he hurried the three visitors into the Throne Room again. Rays of early-morning sun shone through the windows and pierced the gloom. John was surprised to see that the internal decoration of the room was a lot more colourful than he'd realised.

Arranging the three of them facing him, Monkey muttered several words, almost casually. He then tapped the three of them lightly with his staff.

"Well, what are you waiting for?" he asked them. Nervous looks were exchanged between them. "Come on," said Monkey, impatiently. "Let's see you do what I showed you yesterday."

Tommy was the first to try. Holding his arms out behind him as they'd been shown, he gave a little jump into the air. To his amazement, instead of landing on the floor again, he remained about six inches above it.

With a little more effort he managed to move forward and higher, then, by altering his balance and leaning to one side or the other, he found he could turn. It was the strangest feeling he'd ever had, and his face broke into a huge grin as he let out an excited shout. "Wow, this is unbelievable! Auntie, John, come on!"

John and Dotty needed no further bidding and tentatively jumped into the air, whooping with delight when they found that they were hovering. As they became more confident, they tried flying higher. At first it was like dodgems in space, with frequent collisions, both with the walls and each other, but after twenty minutes or so they were reasonably proficient.

"That's enough now, we've got to go!" Monkey's voice brought the fun to an end and steered their minds back to the dangers ahead. They made their way back to the banqueting room, which was now in total chaos as people ran around, shouting orders and waving papers. Lu Shen, who was preparing Wat Su's troops for the march up to the north, wished them luck.

Quickly, they said goodbye, then, stopping only to check they had all the battle orders for the field commanders, they strode out into the courtyard.

Here too was a scene of great activity, with soldiers milling around and horses being saddled for the great day ahead, but everyone stopped to watch the fliers depart. Monkey led the way, followed rather unsteadily by Dotty, John, and finally Tommy. A great cheer rent the air as the four of them rose slowly in the cold morning light.

The four friends headed north. Looking down, they could see people going to work in the fields, as well as columns of soldiers heading towards the frontline all hoping to turn the tide against Boon Kong. The sun was higher in the sky now but the height and speed they were flying kept them cool. Below them, the countryside was a swathe of green interlaced with rivers, which snaked through it. Occasionally, small rocky outcrops jutted up, and as they gently receded again, terraces of paddy fields could be seen.

It was impossible to speak, so they flew along, all thinking their private thoughts, and trying to keep up with Monkey. John was reminded of the time he had been on the back of his father's old motorbike. He'd felt excited as the cold air rushed into his face during the ride, and he felt the same surge of excitement and happiness as he flew alongside his friends. Turning, he smiled at Tommy, and was rewarded by a smile back. It was the start of a long, but hopefully successful day.

CHAPTER 19

After about an hour or so, Dotty slowly started to lose height. Alarmed, the others dropped too, sensing something was wrong. Eventually she landed very badly on the side of a hill. Monkey landed and rushed to Dotty, while the boys thumped to Earth, rolling over several times harmlessly. By the time they reached Dotty, Monkey was already cradling her head in his lap. Her face and hands were blue with cold, her teeth were chattering and the rest of her body shaking uncontrollably. She was close to passing out. Tommy and John were devastated when they saw her.

"Don't worry, boys," said Monkey, reaching behind the breastplate of his armour and producing the small phial again. "This will sort her out in no time."

Gently lifting her head, he urged her to swallow a mouthful of the strange concoction. She managed a little, and though it caused her to cough violently, in less than ten seconds the colour had returned to her cheeks. In no time at all, she looked as if she could take on all Boon Kong's army single-handedly.

"Give me the recipe for that stuff," she said to Monkey, "I could make a fortune!"

Standing up once more, Dotty stretched. "Come on … What are we waiting for?" she goaded the others.

"Not so fast my dear," said Monkey gently. "You may feel as if you can fly up to the sun, but you can't. Just let the potion work in your body for a little longer before we go." Dotty paced up and down impatiently, waiting for the signal to leave. When he was satisfied that it was safe to go, they took off once more with Monkey peering over his shoulder often to make sure Dotty was all right.

After what seemed like a few minutes, Monkey pointed earthward and the others peered down at the first of Wat Su's camps. Straightening, Monkey stretched his arms out ahead and angled down towards the camp at incredible speed.

By the time the rest of them were over the camp, Monkey had already flown up to rejoin them, having delivered the orders to the commander. Far below, about two hundred or so soldiers milled around, pointing and waving at the travellers. Tommy tried to wave back, but the result was disastrous— he was thrown off balance and shot off at an angle from the others. Luckily, he instantly managed to correct his mistake, so was unharmed though shaken.

Wat Su's camps began appearing more frequently as they travelled north, and Monkey had his work cut out, diving down and back up again delivering the orders.

Some time later, they flew over another army but this time the upturned faces were not friendly, and the sun glinting off their copper armour almost blinded the fliers. Instead of waves, they could see outstretched arms pointing urgently in their direction, and could almost sense the hostility even at that distance. John felt a shiver travel down his spine, as the realisation that Boon Kong's soldiers would do all they could to prevent the fliers from achieving their mission struck him anew.

Tommy, also in a serious frame of mind, started thinking about how precious life was, and how his insistent heartbeat sounded to him like the most wonderful sound in the world.

The day was much warmer by the time the northern mountain range became visible. Great jagged peaks thrust up into the clouds, dotted here and there with a few trees and bushes that had managed to secure a perilous footing. Winding its way slowly through the middle of the hostile landscape was a single footpath. They kept it in sight as they flew far above.

As they reached the smaller peaks, Monkey pointed to something up ahead. They peered through the thickening mist and made out the grey outline of the castle. It was an ugly building, which had been built not for looks but for a purpose. It looked impenetrable and even the upper ramparts, where the towers were, were thick and solid-looking. The castle was constructed from massive blocks of stone, which would have been almost impossible to dislodge with conventional weapons. Boon Kong had obviously known what he was doing when he built it.

Up until that moment, the four fliers had been hidden from sight by the mist, but with no warning, the mist parted as they were heading for the battlements.

CHAPTER 20

Boon Kong's Fortress, Northern Provinces, Ancient China

10th September 650 AD

They were spotted immediately by the eagle-eyed guards below, who began shouting excitedly and pointing at them. Monkey gained height quickly gesturing for the others to follow, which they did as best they could. Spurred on by the arrows, which were now whistling towards them, Dotty and the boys dodged about in mid-air.

Then, just when they thought they were out of range, they were suddenly hit by a blast of incredibly hot air, more intense than if they were standing over an open oven door.

"Look out—dragons!" shouted Monkey. John, Tommy and Dotty could not believe their eyes. It's one thing to read about dragons, or to talk about them as some kind of abstract beings, but to experience them at first-hand was another matter altogether.

The three beasts were huge: about twenty feet long and ten feet tall with massive teeth. The dragons' bodies were covered in thick scales, ranging in colour from dark green to deep purple. Sheets of flame shot from their mouths and their swishing tails uprooted bushes, while their claws dug craters in the ground. The three time travellers were all shaken by this sight. The display of naked, mindless force was very frightening.

Monkey pointed urgently to the range of hills at the rear of the castle. Behind them were the mines. As quickly as they could, they headed that way and descended behind a ridge, out of sight of the mine guards.

"I think we'd better try to find the pandas first and set them free," said Monkey. "One of us can distract the guards, while the rest attack them from behind.""I'll distract them," said John, "they won't know what to make of me!"

Having decided on their plan, the other three remained hidden while John stood up and slowly walked over the ridge towards the guards. At first they didn't see him as they were playing some kind of gambling game, but as the game came to an end, one of them looked up and spotted him. Yelling in alarm, the guard tried to stand up while pulling his sword from its scabbard. In his rush, he fell over backwards and knocked into the pot of soup suspended over a fire. Clouds of scalding steam enveloped all of them and it took them precious seconds to organise themselves again.

Although they were now all shouting at John, he kept walking slowly towards them. Another guard raised his spear, but it was obvious they were terrified of John, as they had never seen a boy who looked like him before.

Not wanting to risk being attacked, John stopped moving. The guards, more confident now that he had frozen in his tracks, all raised their spears and started to walk towards him.

John stood his ground but he was unsure of what he should do next. Panic set in as the men drew closer. Where were the others? What were they doing? He had deliberately refrained from looking around for them, in case the guards noticed and spotted them too soon, so he had no idea if help was close by.

He needn't have worried. Just as he was about to make a run for it, Monkey appeared behind the guards. With a sound like a howling wind, and before they could even turn to see what had caused it, Monkey dealt them all a blow on the back of the neck with his staff—one of the few areas on their bodies not protected by armour. They collapsed silently in a heap. On seeing this, Dotty and Tommy made their way quickly down the rocky hillside towards the treadmill and mine.

"Quick!" said Monkey, "now for the pandas." Rushing across to the treadmill, they heaved open the door. Inside were two skeletal pandas, which were barely strong enough to keep moving.

Working together, they managed to coax the creatures outside, where they collapsed onto the ground. Monkey strode over to one of the guards, and shook him roughly to rouse him. "Where are the other pandas?" he demanded.

"There's only another two, in that cage over there," said the guard, indicating a small cage, which was fully exposed to the sun's rays. The smell that hit them as they approached almost stopped them in their tracks, but they persisted, opening the cage up and dragging out the two occupants. Dried saliva caked their jaws and swollen tongues protruded between their teeth. Their eyes barely registered anything as they were manhandled out of the cage.

"Where are the fresh bamboo shoots?" Monkey asked.

"In that cave over there," replied the guard.

"Dotty, go and get some shoots and see if you can get the pandas to eat." Monkey turned back to the guard again. "Where are the other pandas? We were told ten were still alive."

"Six died this week and we've fed them to the dragons!" blubbered the guard.

Returning with an armful of bamboo shoots, Dotty gently tried to get the animals to open their mouths and take a little food but she had no success. It seemed the pandas were just too weak, and had given up on life.

"I think they've had it," said John. Fortunately for the starving beasts, Tommy looked down at the scene, he had a brainwave. "Monkey, have you got any more of that stuff left you gave Dotty this morning?" he asked.

"A little," said Monkey.

"Let's try it on the pandas!"

"Yes, why not?" said John, "I don't think anything else will work now."

Monkey scratched his head. "I've never used it on pandas before ..." he said. "It might do more harm than good, but then again, we haven't much choice." Reaching into his pocket he produced the little phial, and very gently tipped a few drops down the throat of the panda Dotty was trying to feed. Nothing happened for a few seconds, then gradually its eyes opened wider, and its jaws started to move.

"Quick," said Tommy, "offer it some bamboo!" This time there was a difference. The animal sniffed the shoots and nibbled gently at them. "Well done Tommy!" whispered Dotty, "let's hope they'll respond this way!"

CHAPTER 21

Boon Kong's Kingdom, Northern Provinces, Ancient China

10th September 650 AD

Turning back to the guard once again, Monkey managed to extract the information that six other guards were on duty.

"You stay here and try to get the pandas to eat, while I'll get this guard to show me where the others are," he said. "One of you had better keep a look out, just in case he's lying and there are more."

The guard led Monkey to the entrance to the mine, where they encountered two other guards who'd been sent to see why the pump had stopped working. Monkey raised his staff and headed towards them as they drew swords from their sheaths. The guard Monkey had brought with him, seeing a chance, stopped and reached into his armour.

"Look out!"

Monkey heard John's shout and spun round in time to see the guard about to lash out with a dagger.

"You get those two, I'll deal with this one," shouted John, running up to them.

Monkey had no time to argue, and moved into a position where he could hit them with his staff.

Meanwhile, John had drawn his dagger, and was circling the first guard. His mind was working overtime, trying to remember all that he'd been taught about fighting with a dagger. He'd had a few scraps in the playground, but this was for real. He knew that this man would kill him if he got the chance.

John, however, had no stomach to try to kill somebody even if, technically, they had died centuries before he was born. The guard lunged at him, grunting as he did so. John feinted from one side to the other, desperately dodging the flashing blade, until, suddenly, the guard's foot landed on a small stone, causing him to lose his balance for an instant. As quick as a flash, John dived to the ground and stabbed the man as hard as he could in both calves, which were unprotected. The guard screamed with pain and collapsed to the ground, clutching at his legs, which were now streaming with blood.

Seeing the damage he had caused, John felt ill. He wished he could say something to the man to make him understand that he had not really wanted to hurt him. His thoughts were interrupted, however, by Monkey shouting at him to give him a hand.

Turning, John ran towards his friend. The sight of the blond-haired boy clutching a bloodstained dagger made the other guards lose their concentration for a moment, which was all it took. Monkey lunged at one and caught him a glancing blow to the side of the head with his staff, which sent him reeling. On seeing this, the other guard turned and fled back down the tunnel, shouting loudly as he did so.

"Quick John, we must get him," shouted Monkey. They chased after the escapee, but he had the advantage both in knowing the twisting maze of tunnels and having eyes that were accustomed to the gloom. He soon lost them, vanishing like a rabbit down one of the many small side tunnels.

"*Kazambah!*" cried Monkey in frustration. "We won't waste any more time trying to find him."

By this time, their eyes were used to the dim light and they could make out a much wider area ahead, which had several cages in it, similar to the ones the pandas had been in.

Cautiously they made their way towards them. Inside crouched several ragged people.

"Help us, help us!" one whispered. The call was picked up by the others, so that within minutes the walls were echoing with the pleading of several dozen people. "Help us, let us out. We want to go back to our fields and families."

"Who are they?" whispered John to Monkey.

"The villagers that Boon Kong imprisoned to work here," replied Monkey, striking the chains that bound the cages with his staff. There was a flash of light, which made several women scream and back away. But, they all fell silent when the chains fell to the floor and the cage-fronts dropped open. At first, nobody dared make a move. Monkey, however, spoke softly to them and coaxed them out, telling them that their help was needed to stop Boon Kong's hold on the kingdom.

Quickly, he explained to them that the plan was to penetrate the castle and defeat Boon Kong. One of the prisoners tugged at Monkey's sleeve. "Excuse me, Excellency, but I feel there is something you should know," he said. "Boon Kong was here two days ago with two other men, one of whom looked like him." The man pointed to John.

"What about the other stranger, what did he look like?" enquired Monkey.

"He was like us, but wore very strange clothes and shoes like the other, and when they spoke, it was in a strange language."

"It must have been Ferret-Teeth and his friend!" said John, without hesitation.

"I think so too," said Monkey, "and if they have managed to come back here, their magic may be very powerful. We must hurry to the castle at once." Straightening, he was starting to usher everyone to the mine entrance, when the prisoner who had just spoken stopped him.

"There is a connecting passage to the castle," he said. "Boon Kong and the others came and left from tunnels that lead deeper into the mine."

"This is just what we suspected," cried Monkey. "Ching Lai told us that there was a secret passage too. If we can find it, we can regain the element of surprise. Do any of you know where it is?" asked Monkey. Everyone shook their heads. Monkey stamped his foot, angry that the chance seemed to be slipping away.

"What about the guard?" cried John. Monkey flashed a grin at him before whirling around. Luckily, the guard John had crippled was still lying where they had left him.

"Where's the tunnel to the castle?" Monkey shouted. "If you don't tell us, I'll let the prisoners decide your fate. I bet they've got several ways of getting rid of you that would take hours!"

The guard looked terrified. "No, please …" he begged.

"Quickly then," said Monkey.

"I'll have to show you," said the guard. "It's too complicated to try and tell you. But I can't walk, so someone will have to carry me."

CHAPTER 22

Boon Kong's Kingdom, Northern Provinces, Ancient China

10th September 650 AD

Saying nothing, Monkey reached for the small phial in his tunic, put some of the dark liquid onto his fingers, and rubbed it into the wounds on the guard's legs. Instantly the bleeding stopped, and the guard was able to stand up with no trouble.

"Right, let's go. I want the youngest and fittest prisoners to come with us. The rest of you, go and look after the pandas. Be as gentle as you can with them and try to get them to eat. Someone must stay with them the whole time. If the last of them die, we're all finished, as the gods will destroy the whole Kingdom. Then all your suffering will have been for nothing. Send the woman and the boy you meet to us."

Before long, they heard footsteps as Dotty and Tommy came running down the tunnel to join them. Monkey beckoned the guard to show them the way, and the man set off, glancing back fearfully at Monkey and the others from time to time. Occasionally he stopped at the point where the tunnels met or divided to make sure he was taking the right one.

"Do not cross me," warned Monkey, "because you know who I am and what I will do."

The guard nodded fearfully. "Yes Excellency, you can trust me, I will do as you say."

Eventually they reached the entrance to the castle. There was a thick wooden door, covered in a thin sheet of Boon Kong's special copper. Monkey and Dotty tried to turn the circular metal handle, but nothing happened. There was nothing else on the surface of the door, so Monkey guessed that the locking mechanism was on the other side. It seemed as though they would have to retrace their steps and then try to gain access to the castle from the battlements, but just as he was about to wearily tell the others to turn back, Monkey spotted an axe lying by a pile of wood just down the tunnel. Seizing it with a cry, he swung it into the door with all his might.

The axe bounced straight back and flew from his hands as if the door had been made of rubber.

Angered, he hit it with his staff. There was a huge flash when the staff made contact, but again it flew from his grasp and landed on the ground by the axe.

Monkey's eyes flashed.

Just then, his super-sensitive hearing picked up a small noise. He motioned to the others to keep quiet and strained his ears. Almost casually, he picked up his staff and tapped the guard on the head causing him to fall down, unconscious.

"Just in case he tried to warn them," said Monkey.

"Warn who?" asked Tommy, echoed by Dotty.

"Whoever is coming down the secret passage!" said Monkey.

Sure enough, they soon heard the sound of bolts being withdrawn, and locks being undone, along with muffled voices.

Quickly, they flattened themselves against the cold damp walls, as the door opened slowly. First one guard, then another came through.

As they turned to close the door behind them, Monkey sprang out, and, faster than the eye could see, tapped them both on the back of the neck. He then shot through the still-open door and did the same to the guard on the other side. As the final guard collapsed, Dotty spotted a long metal object on the ground, which had fallen from his hand.

"This must be the door key!" she said.

Single file, they proceeded up the narrow passage. Monkey led the way, followed by John then Dotty, with Tommy taking up the rear. Behind him were the dozen or so prisoners who had been strong enough to join them.

After about ten minutes, they reached another door. Monkey pressed his ear to it and listened intently.

"What can you hear?" hissed Dotty.

"Ssshh!" hissed Monkey, twisting his face with the effort of listening. "I must make sure that no one is around, otherwise we'll lose the element of surprise."

Gently he pushed the door, only to discover it had been locked.

"Pass me that key, Dotty," he said. "Let's see if it opens these doors." Luckily, the notched metal bar slid in and turned smoothly.

Very, very gently, Monkey opened the door, listening intently all the while. Silently he motioned the others to follow him out into the dim passageway. "Who can remember the plan of the castle?" he asked them.

"I can do better than tell you—I can show you!" said Tommy. "I got the plan from Ching Lai before we left." He produced the small map and passed it to Monkey, who surveyed it quickly, grunting quietly as he did so.

"I think we go this way," he said, indicating a short passageway in the dungeons. It ran from the cells, past several small rooms with locked doors, to a flight of stairs leading to the inner courtyard.

CHAPTER 23

Northern Provinces, Ancient China

10ᵗʰ September 650 AD

"Let's head for the armour room," said Monkey. They proceeded warily down the short passageway and were met by the sight of three guards seated round a table, with the cells on either side of them. Past them lay the steps and the massive, copper reinforced door to the armour room.

Before anyone else had time to think or say anything, Monkey had sprung onto the table with a single bound, causing the guards to jump up in surprise. One of them lost his balance and fell to the floor. Seizing his chance, Monkey tapped him with his staff. The other two made a dash for the passage, but before they could escape, one was struck by Monkey and the other was overpowered by the former prisoners that Monkey had recruited. As they started releasing the prisoners locked in the cells, a lance embedded itself in the table with great force.

Scattering, they looked up to see where it had come from. There was a general gasp of amazement. What the plan had not shown was that the guard room was at the bottom of a huge shaft, which ran straight down through the middle of one of the castle turrets.

There, up above them, peering over the side from different levels, were dozens of soldiers and servants, and, right near the top, three figures.

"Oh no! That's Ferret-Teeth up there!" cried Tommy. By this time the soldiers had started firing arrows, as well as hurling their lances. Everyone down below threw themselves out of the way, some dashing into the open cells, others back into the passageway. The prisoners were terrified and screamed at Monkey to help them. In their haste to escape the hail of missiles, they knocked over a large container of water, making the floor very slippery.

Monkey and the time travellers scrambled up the steps and squeezed close to the copper door for protection.

Dotty tried the key she'd taken from the guard in the door, but it wouldn't turn. Suddenly she saw another similar key lying near the table, about six feet away.

"The key we need is there!" she hissed. Without hesitation, Tommy darted out and dived under the table, attracting a renewed barrage of arrows. Biding his time, he tried to judge when it would be safe to stretch out his arm and retrieve the key, but the missiles came thick and fast. He began to wish he'd stayed put, when John suddenly came crashing into him.

"What are you doing?" shouted Tommy.

John explained that together they could probably lift the heavy table on their shoulders and move it to where the key was, before making their way back to the door.

With John at the front and Tommy at the back, they

strained to lift the heavy wooden table in the air. Like a giant drunken tortoise they staggered over the few feet to the key, and gratefully lowered the table.

Picking up the key, Tommy threw it across to Dotty who tried to fit it in the lock. She jiggled and twisted, but it would not go in.

Monkey lost patience. He felt they were making no headway by playing it safe. The time had come for him to take action. Silently, he took a deep breath and steeled himself. He knew what the consequences would be for the action he was about to take.

With a blood-chilling yell he launched himself from the steps, spinning almost faster than the eye could follow. As he rose up the shaft, his staff emitted a beam of intense white light, which he directed at the soldiers' faces. They dropped their weapons and clutched their eyes as the powerful beam hit them. Those on the higher levels, seeing what was happening, fled for their lives.

Right at the top, Boon Kong smashed his clenched fists into the parapet he was looking over. His face contorted with rage, making him look monstrous. Sweat poured from his face, making dark patches on his tunic collar. The effort of racing up the stairs with his damaged leg had made his mood worse than ever.

"Those interfering idiots!" he screamed. "I will not allow them to ruin all my years of work and planning."

Seeing that Monkey was getting uncomfortably close to the top, Ferret-Teeth touched Boon Kong's shoulder and murmured, "We'd better go, there's no point in trying to stop him here. It will merely drain us of our magic. Better to save it for later, when he's spent."

"All right," growled Boon Kong, but he couldn't leave without leaning over the parapet one final time to bellow, "Mark my words, this is the beginning of the end for you!" Then turning back, he and his two companions strode away.

When Monkey was sure that he had cleared the whole shaft of attackers, he descended again, and told the prisoners to run down the tunnel and join the others at the mine.

"That was incredible!" said Dotty, "why didn't you do that before?"

"Because it comes with a high price. I shall now be powerless for about an hour," explained Monkey. "That was a weapon of desperation." John and Tommy crawled out from under the table and helped Dotty fit the key in the armour-room door.

"I think it moved a bit!" said John. "You pull on the handle while I try again." Tommy grasped the handle and tugged as hard as he could, while John frantically forced the key into the hole.

"It's in!" he cried, twisting it as hard as he could.

"Stop, you'll break it!" shouted Dotty, but it was too late. As the words left her mouth, the key snapped in half leaving the lock well and truly jammed.

"No!" yelled Tommy, "now we'll never get in!"

"But nor will they," said Monkey.

CHAPTER 24

Northern Provinces, Ancient China

10ᵗʰ September 650 AD

"What do we do now? We can't stay here," said Dotty, "we're like rats in a trap. Let's fly up to the top and see if we can find a way out."

"You can, but I can't," said Monkey.

"What do you mean?" asked Dotty, incredulously.

"My antics a few minutes ago have left me powerless for a while … Which means I cannot fly."

"Oh," said Dotty, with genuine concern. "Well we can't go without you. Can you walk to the top?"

"I think so," replied Monkey. At his words, Tommy and John, who had been itching to get out of the dank guard area, raced off.

Glancing anxiously upwards as they went, Dotty and Monkey followed them past the cells and into the tunnel, where Monkey gestured to them to stop.

"Listen very carefully, Tommy," said Monkey, "this is where your role comes in. You remember I told you that we might need you to represent the accumulated wisdom and goodness of the future generations?" Tommy nodded. "Well," Monkey continued, "I'm powerless for about the next three quarters of an hour, and Boon Kong probably knows that. I was hoping that we wouldn't need to do this, but because his magical allies from the future are here too, we don't have a choice. You must trust me completely, and do whatever I tell you without question. Do you understand?"

Tommy nodded gravely, his little face unable to mask the fear he was feeling.

"What I'm going to do is to fill you with my knowledge, so whatever happens, you will know what to do."

"I don't understand," said Tommy.

"There is no way," continued Monkey, "that I can *teach* you enough magic, so instead I'm going to *transfer* my knowledge into your mind. That means that you will know and be able to recite any spells you need without thinking!"

Monkey patted Tommy's shoulder to reassure him, then held one end of his staff up to his right eye, gesturing for Tommy to hold the other end up to his. For a good two minutes they stood there, Tommy's face occasionally twisting, as an incredible amount of power and knowledge passed across to him. When it was over, he collapsed onto the floor of the tunnel.

Monkey knelt by him, muttering softly and gently massaging Tommy's temples with his thumbs. Suddenly, Tommy sat bolt upright and opened his eyes. The others gasped in amazement.

Gone were Tommy's soft brown eyes, and in their place was a

pair of hard, glinting, steel-like orbs.

"What have you done to him?" cried Dotty in horror, unable to control herself.

"Don't worry," said Monkey, "it's not permanent."

"What's not permanent?" said Tommy, in a voice so loud that he made himself jump and the others back away from him in terror. "What have you done to me?" he repeated. The mighty roar shook the walls of the tunnel and went swirling up to the top of the shaft.

"Shh …" said Monkey, "don't worry … trust me."

Taking Tommy's hand, Dotty said, "Monkey's brought us this far, let's trust him to get us safely back."

Monkey nodded gratefully to Dotty, and then said to Tommy, "No matter what Boon Kong does, you must let the words and actions flow out of you naturally, don't try to resist them. Don't say anything now, just nod or shake your head to show you understand." Tommy nodded. "Even if it feels very strange and uncomfortable, you must try to relax as much as possible, and whatever you do, don't stop halfway through a spell!"

Tommy felt slightly calmer after Monkey had talked to him and he silently promised only to communicate with the others by nodding his head.

"Right," said Monkey, "I think the best thing we can do now is to get to the top of the castle."

Cautiously, he approached the stairs and listened intently. He couldn't hear anything, apart from the occasional groan coming from the victims of his earlier sortie. He motioned to the others to join him, and together they climbed the spiral stairs.

Each time they reached a new level, they found a small room. Most had Boon Kong's soldiers lying in a heap, caught by Monkey's attack only minutes before.

After slow but steady progress they finally reached the top level, where they'd seen Boon Kong and Ferret-Teeth. There was no trace of them now, however. Cautiously, they crept down a narrow passageway lit by a tallow candle, which had been stuck in a holder made from a panda's foot. Seeing the holder upset John.

"What kind of people are they?" he whispered to Dotty. "I want to make sure they can never do stuff like this again."

At the end of the passage was a locked door. Monkey did not even bother to look for a key. Instead, he told the others to back away and told Tommy to let his mind go blank.

He hissed several words into Tommy's ear then stood back. After a few seconds, Tommy's face contorted, and the terrible booming voice they'd heard earlier burst out of his lungs. The door shook violently, then quivered, and was still.

"Fat lot of good that was!" said John, before he could stop himself. Saying nothing, Monkey took John's hand in his paw and led him to the door. Taking John's index finger he placed it gently on the door, and it disintegrated in front of their eyes, dropping into a pile of dust at their feet. John's face made his apology for him.

The door led onto the battlements. Cautiously, they ventured through it, and felt the fresh air on their hot faces.

Peering around the corner, Monkey spotted several guards looking over the battlements, apparently watching the dragons below. He signalled the others back inside and whispered his plan to them. One by one, the time travellers crept through the door then dropped over the edge of the battlements, flying along beneath the guards, out of their sight, until they were stationed beneath the three furthest guards.

When the others were positioned where he wanted them, Monkey leapt onto the battlements with a loud shout. The guards turned to look at him, and as they did so, the others rose up behind them and pulled them over the top. Monkey sprang at the one nearest him and pushed him down into the inner courtyard, where he landed at the back of a large dung heap.

Just then Monkey's sensitive hearing picked up a cry from the ridge below, behind which were the mines and pandas. Squinting down, he spotted a villager waving frantically.

"Quick Tommy, go and see what the matter is," said Monkey.

"But I won't be able to understand him!" boomed Tommy, causing the dragons to look up and cower.

"You will. Trust me," said Monkey with a smile.

Tommy flew off at speed. Instantly there were shouts from below as he was spotted by several guards, who'd now found the toppled guards at the foot of the wall. Several arrows zinged past but Tommy dodged them with ease.

Swiftly, he dived behind the ridge, only to reappear a split-second later, furiously beckoning the others to follow. They rose straight up into the air, and luckily, as he'd regained a lot of his strength and powers, Monkey was able to join them. The arrows didn't come close, but as they passed above the outside wall, they were suddenly alerted to a new danger by a blast of searingly hot air.

"Cover your mouths and noses," shouted Monkey, "and don't look down at the dragons!" John and Dotty felt their lungs would explode with the tremendous heat of the dragons' fiery breath. The dragons were fortunately tethered with special chains, and could not follow them.

CHAPTER 25

Northern Provinces, Ancient China

10th September 650 AD

In no time at all, they were past the danger and were reunited with Tommy.

"The villagers have just told me that Boon Kong and Ferret-Teeth have come through the tunnel to the mines," thundered Tommy.

"He'll probably try and finish the pandas off!" cried Dotty.

"Either that, or he'll try and use them as bargaining tools," said Monkey. "He probably realises he can't win now and will want to salvage what he can."

As they were speaking, they reached the edge of the ridge. Peering down onto the area where the pandas had been, they saw utter chaos down there. Boon Kong was limping around, lashing out as if he was trying to get the villagers and pandas back into the cages again. Ferret-Teeth and his Chinese friend were there too, together with several guards. Both the villagers and pandas were resisting capture, and were now much livelier after having been given the potion and some food. As soon as a panda was seized, the others would attack the guards. Suddenly, Boon Kong shouted, "Enough! Just kill them all, and let's go."

"This is it," said Monkey, "we've got to go down now, or everything will have been for nothing." He rose up from behind the rocks and led the others down into the clearing, opposite the cages.

"Monkey! We meet at last," said Boon Kong. "You and your band of misfits are about to experience the power of real magic, not your cheap conjuring tricks!" He waved his arms and a dragon appeared in front of them, clawing at the earth, flames leaping from its nostrils.

"Stay calm, it's an illusion," Monkey whispered. He turned, said a few words and waved his arms. The large dragon turned into a tiny mouse which ran off, squeaking. Boon Kong was noticeably alarmed at this turn of events, and muttered something to his henchmen.

Together, the evil trio recited an incantation. The pandas suddenly changed into sparrows, and flew away up into the hills.

"Oh no! I'll say a spell to keep them safe," said Monkey, "while Tommy concentrates on getting rid of those three." Again he spoke to Tommy, who started loudly reciting a spell. When Boon Kong and the others heard the spell he was casting, a look of disbelief crossed their faces.

"If you use that spell," Boon Kong shouted, "you'll destroy everything — including yourselves."

"With the pandas gone, we are facing destruction anyway," replied Monkey. "And this way, you won't escape either."

With a curse, Boon Kong whirled around and snarled something. Hastily, Ferret-Teeth fumbled at his jacket pocket and produced the bowl and chopsticks.

Boon Kong had calculated that they would just about have enough time to travel in time and escape before Tommy finished the spell.

As Ferret-Teeth and friend were busying themselves with the bowl, Boon Kong started to recite spells of his own. From out of nowhere, a huge swarm of bees suddenly descended on the time travellers, each bee several times bigger than any they had ever seen. The angry buzzing was horrendous and despite Monkey yelling, "They're only an illusion," John and Dotty just couldn't help flailing their arms about. Even Tommy's recitation started to falter as he became aware of the giant insects.

Monkey was in a dilemma. He couldn't get rid of the bees on his own, but he didn't dare stop Tommy, because then he'd have to start the first spell again, completely from scratch.

Whilst he was considering what to do, a dozen scorpions appeared at their feet, their stinging tails poised menacingly above their heads. Dotty screamed—there was only so much she could stand.

"Listen to me," said Monkey. "What we are seeing is not real, they can't hurt us. Just tell yourself that, and hold on, don't let him win!"

Boon Kong, witnessing the confusion he had caused, smiled. He barked an order at Ferret-Teeth, who had the bowl and chopsticks ready. All three of them joined hands, and touched the ends of the chopsticks.

Hurriedly, he began to recite the incantation, but far more

quickly than Dotty had done.

"But, you can't take three into the bowl," whispered Dotty. "Doesn't he realise that?"

Even as she spoke, Boon Kong and the Chinese man started to dematerialise and flow down into the chopsticks. "Maybe it does work after all," said Dotty, watching as the effect spread to Ferret-Teeth in the middle.

Just then, something strange happened. Most of Ferret-Teeth's body had flowed into the chopsticks and just one leg was left standing, when suddenly the flow stopped.

"You were right!" said Monkey. "It can't cope, and his leg is left behind! Not only that, they haven't managed to go back to your time, either!"

"Why not?" chorused John and Dotty.

"Because the chopsticks are the wrong way round! To go forward in time you must have the thicker ends touching, not the points. They're going to go back in time now!"

As they continued to watch, the chopsticks glowed and flowed up into the bowl, which in turn glowed, and then faded from sight. Soon, all that was left was Ferret-Teeth's leg!

Monkey now turned back to Tommy and shook him, to get him to stop saying the spell. However, this was easier said than done, as he was in a trance-like state and was taking Monkey's instructions to let nothing distract him very seriously.

"We have to do something!" said Dotty. "Is it true what Boon Kong said about this spell destroying everything?"

"Yes, I'm afraid it is," said Monkey, "and he's almost finished it!"

"What he needs is a good shock!" said Dotty.

She sent John across to where Ferret-Teeth's leg stood and made him pick it up. John's nose wrinkled with disgust as he struggled back with the strange object. Seizing it, Dotty waved the leg in front of Tommy's face. "Tommy, Tommy, look, it's Ferret-Teeth's leg. He's gone, Boon Kong's gone. Stop the spell!"

Tommy's eyes started to register the movement and the terrible voice faltered, until he gradually became aware of what Dotty was saying to him. His voice trailed off as he realised his aunt was waving around a human leg!

"That was too close for comfort," said Monkey, as Dotty gratefully dropped the leg on the ground.

"Auntie?" asked Tommy in his own voice.

"Oh, thank goodness you're back to normal." Dotty took hold of Tommy and gave him a hug, planting a big kiss on top of his head.

CHAPTER 26

Northern Provinces, Ancient China

10th September 650 AD

"Well done, Tommy. Now all we have to do is to get the pandas back," said Monkey, smiling.

"How do we do that?" said Tommy.

"I have to summon all the birds down here, like this," said Monkey, emitting a curious high-pitched note, which was a cross between a warble and a whistle. John had just reappeared after rounding up the freed villagers and everybody watched silently as the sky darkened, and several hundred birds descended onto the ground around them.

"I have to call them all," said Monkey, "because they have to be on the ground, you see, before I change them back to pandas again. Just imagine what would happen if one were to change back perched on a branch, or even flying!" He looked at his captive audience, obviously relishing the chance to show off. "Now I must talk to them," he said.

Monkey then allowed each species in turn to fly off. The hawks, finches, crows, magpies, eagles, and every other type of bird except sparrows, were eliminated. There were about two dozen sparrows left. He asked all of them whether they knew each other.

By a process of elimination he was eventually left with three birds; but there had been four pandas! Monkey turned to Dotty. "What shall I do now? I don't know where the missing one is. If it's still flying or up in a tree, the fall will kill it when I change them back."

As they spoke, a large hawk-like bird appeared from the direction of the castle, flying away from them. It was carrying something in its talons.

"Why didn't that bird come when you called all the others?" John asked Monkey.

"I don't know, but I intend to find out," said Monkey, as he sped upwards towards it. As he got nearer, he could see the missing sparrow clutched in the bird's cruel grasp.

"Why did you not obey my command?" he asked the bird.

"Since when does the God of the Clouds have to answer to a second-rate god like you, Monkey?" the hawk screeched. "And let me tell you, before you do anything stupid, that our little friend here is the remaining male panda. The sparrows you have are all female."

So that was it, Boon Kong's mentor had decided to show his hand (or claw) at last! Monkey's brain went into overdrive. If what the God of the Clouds said was true, then Monkey had to get the sparrow away from him without harming it. That would be extremely difficult, as just one hard squeeze from those talons would kill it.

"What do you want?" asked Monkey.

"I think you know," replied the God of the Clouds.

"Despite your reputation as a clown, we both know that you are perceptive and clever."

"Let me guess, then," said Monkey. "In return for letting the sparrow go, you want to take Wat Su's Kingdom."

"Well done, Monkey," said the God of the Clouds sarcastically. "I've waited, and worked and planned these many years to gain control of all the earthly lands, and I won't allow a stupid Monkey to steal my prize now!"

During the course of this exchange Monkey had been racking his brains for a way to catch the sparrow. An idea had occurred to him, but it would need a good deal of luck for it to work.

Still, as he had no choice, Monkey quickly recited a spell. He managed to do it so swiftly that it took the God of the Clouds completely by surprise.

Before he could counteract it, the God of the Clouds suddenly found himself turned into a duck. As a duck's webbed feet are no good for grasping things, the little sparrow fell from his grasp.

Monkey shouted at the sparrow to fly to the others, while he and the God of the Clouds settled some old scores.

A few feathers drifted earthwards as the God of the Clouds changed back into his usual form and then attacked Monkey in earnest. From the ground the others saw the missing sparrow arrive safely and land, and then watched in awe as the two gods battled against each other. What a sight it was!

Blinding flashes of light shot down to earth, and mighty crashes, far louder than the worst thunderstorm rent the skies. The God of the Clouds swooped up and behind Monkey, and with a grunt of exertion, he propelled a thunderbolt straight at him. Monkey turned in time to see it coming, and shot out of its way. In return, he flew straight at the God of the Clouds and dealt him a glancing blow with his staff.

"Enough of this!" roared the God of the Clouds. "Your time has come, Monkey. Prepare for your final humiliation." Monkey realised that the God of the Clouds was about to do something desperate. As the God of the Clouds had not been allowed in Heaven for a long time, they should have been evenly matched. But because of his earlier exertions, Monkey was growing tired and could not hold out much longer. Desperately, he broke away and swooped back down to join the others.

"Quick Tommy, come and stand by me and give me help when I tell you!" Tommy rushed to Monkey's side, and at his bidding, gripped his staff as tightly as he could. Quickly, they swung it around and pointed it at the God of the Clouds who was rushing down towards them.

"Now!" yelled Monkey, and both he and Tommy channelled all their power into the staff, which seemed to swell visibly where they touched it. Both their faces were contorted with the effort they were making, and the veins on Tommy's neck stood out alarmingly. Sweat poured from them and Tommy let out several gasps as he felt himself start to lose consciousness. But just as he was about to keel over, the magic finished its journey up the length of the staff to the tip.

With a terrible shrieking noise, the most hideous thing any of them had ever seen burst out of the top of the staff. It reminded John of the gargoyles he'd seen on old churches, but it was far uglier and more evil.

Seeing it, the God of the Clouds immediately stopped in

his tracks, then turned tail and fled. The monstrous creature pursued him until they were both tiny specks high above them in the sky.

"What was that?" whispered Dotty, her shocked expression mirrored in the faces of the others.

"That was all the accumulated evil that Tommy carried with him from all his ancestors."

"What will happen to him now?" asked John.

"If he's lucky, he'll manage to escape and hide. If not, he may try to seek sanctuary in the Imperial Heaven. If he does that, the other gods will probably allow him refuge, but will strip him of all his powers, which will save me a lot of headaches!"

"What will happen to that thing then?" asked Tommy.

"Well, if it catches him, it will destroy him. But it cannot enter the Imperial Heaven; so if he hides there, it will come back to *us*."

Just as the words left Monkey's mouth, they saw the beast reappear and hurtle towards them.

"Oh no!" screamed Dotty, "he must have escaped and now it's coming after us!" Tommy, Dotty and John all clung to each other and closed their eyes waiting for the inevitable, as the terrible roar got louder and closer.

The next second there was the most enormous explosion any of them had ever heard. They were thrown violently off their feet and enveloped in a swirling cloud of dust. Dotty picked herself up and looked for the others. They were all there, but above them the castle was no longer standing. A massive black cloud hung over the wreck. Debris of various sizes started to rain down on them.

"Let's shelter in the mine," shouted Tommy. "Grab the sparrows and Ferret-Teeth's leg." They needed no further bidding. They quickly flew into the entrance, as massive chunks of rock from the castle fell from the sky, smashing the cages and treadmill to pieces. Even a dragon's severed head crashed onto the ground just outside the entrance, its lifeless eyes staring balefully at them.

Eventually, the massive chunks of rock from the ruin stopped falling, and only tiny particles floated down. Monkey announced that it was safe to venture out so they all flew up to see what was left of the castle.

The once-proud fortress had been reduced to a smoking crater, surrounded by flattened trees and piles of stones. It was also eerily quiet. Slowly they descended again, hardly believing what they'd just seen.

CHAPTER 27

Northern Provinces, Ancient China

10th September 650 AD

As the friends slowly landed, they began to realise how tired they were, but they were not able to rest until they knew that the sparrows had been turned back into pandas, and were safe.

Together with the villagers, they wearily formed a large circle with four little sparrows in the middle. Monkey solemnly recited the spell to transform them back into pandas, then they silently waited.

After several minutes had passed, Tommy looked up. The sparrows were still hopping about on the ground. There was no sign of the pandas reappearing. Monkey became anxious. He knew he had to get the time travellers back to Wat Su's palace within three hours, before the sun set and they lost their ability to fly.

Gathering the villagers around him, he explained that the spell would be broken at sunset and that he was sure the birds would change back into pandas. He asked that they take care of the pandas when they reappeared, giving them fresh bamboo shoots and clean water, and generally pampering them in every way.

"What did he say?" asked John curiously.

"He asked them," said Dotty, "to 'pander' to the pandas' every whim!" Tommy and John collapsed into laughter; the first time they'd done so for a while.

When Monkey was sure that the pandas would be properly cared for, he told the others it was time to leave.

"But what about Ferret-Teeth's leg?" asked John. "Are we going to leave it here?"

"No, we'd better bring it with us," said Monkey, "you never know when you might need it."

"What do mean?" asked Tommy.

"Well, if, by chance, Ferret-Teeth manages to return to your time, having his leg would give you something to bargain with, if he threatens you."

"But how am I going to explain a leg to my parents?" wailed Tommy.

"Don't worry," said Monkey reassuringly. "I'll reduce it in size so that you can hide it somewhere safe. If Ferret-Teeth ever comes back, you can let him have his leg in exchange for him leaving you alone. There are ways of making sure this arrangement works. Let me deal with it now, then we must get going."

Swiftly, Monkey flew in the direction of the mine, returning a little while later. Grinning widely, he pulled the now tiny leg out of the pocket of his tunic. It was encased in a thin layer of crystal. "This will protect it for now," said Monkey, giving them a wink.

Now it really was time to go, and so, with a final wave to the villagers they all soared up into the sky. As they flew swiftly back home, they saw Boon Kong's troops in disarray, leaving the battlegrounds in bedraggled groups. It seemed they had lost the will to fight.

The further south they went, the lower they flew, and Wat Su's men gave them a rousing cheer each time they flew over. By the time they'd reached their destination, the last glimmer of sun had almost gone. Wat Su's palace seemed to be deserted.

However, when they landed in the inner courtyard, they were immediately surrounded by guards, who, on recognising the intruders, broke into loud cheering. Faces appeared at the palace windows, and before long, Wat Su and Chou Ping had rushed out into the courtyard.

Although they were now almost asleep on their feet, the travellers wearily gave a very brief account of the day's events to Wat Su and Chou Ping.

Wat Su waited only long enough to hear that everything had gone well, and then sent everyone off for a hot bath and a good night's sleep. Soon, only Monkey and Wat Su were left in the Throne Room, toasting the day's great success.

CHAPTER 28

Prince Wat Su's Palace, Southern Provinces, Ancient China

10th September 650 AD

The next morning it was time to say goodbye. The time travellers were dressed in their own clothes once again. The boys were excited at the thought of getting back to their own time again, as the computer version of Dungeons and Dragons they played at home was far more attractive than the version they'd just endured for real.

"Well boys," said Dotty "I think that as soon as we've said our goodbyes, we'll get the bowl and chopst..." Her voice faded, with the realisation that she no longer had the bowl and chopsticks in her possession.

Tommy and John, who'd been struck by the same thought, looked at each other in horror. Did this mean that they'd be stuck in Ancient China for the rest of their lives?

Interesting though it had been, they all were desperate to get back to their own time. Apart from anything else, their respective families would be wondering what had happened to them.

"What's the matter, my young friends?" laughed Monkey. "Are you tired of us so soon? We have several more jobs you can help us with ... Surely you're not in a rush to get back?"

The time travellers looked uncomfortable. Had they been tricked into helping Wat Su and Monkey?

Tommy was just about to launch into a protest, when Monkey gave them a sly grin. "What's the matter with all of you? I thought you all enjoyed a good joke." Walking over to a small side table, he removed a cover. Underneath were the bowl and chopsticks!

"How did you get them back?" asked Dotty in amazement.

"We didn't," said Monkey. "This set belongs to Chou Ping. Now, before you go, I must tell you a few things. Firstly, I have written for each of you a set of precise instructions on how to bargain with Ferret-Teeth if he ever returns. Secondly, when you return to your time you won't remember anything about this little trip at all. But I've made sure that if Ferret-Teeth does come back, you will automatically know what to do." He handed them each a piece of paper. "I want you all to spend the next few minutes carefully reading these instructions, then return them to me."

Monkey watched as they read what he'd written and then dutifully handed the papers back to him.

"Why shouldn't we remember anything about this?" asked Tommy.

"It's better if you don't, for all sorts of reasons," said Monkey, "not least of which is that it could drive you mad thinking about it."

"Yes, I can see that," said Dotty thoughtfully. Monkey

suggested that John should be the one to keep the leg safe. "I've disguised it as a tourist trinket from a small island to the north of your country," he said, proudly handing over a pendant. John looked at it curiously. The pendant, which was covered in a thin layer of Boon Kong's special copper, was shaped like three legs joined at the thigh. The legs were bent and arranged in a Y shape. John held it up to the light and grinned.

"Brilliant, it's the symbol of the Isle of Man!" said John.

"You won't remember what it is, of course, but you will know never to let it out of your sight. One day your life may depend on it! Now it is time to say our goodbyes."

The time travellers briefly embraced Wat Su, Chou Ping, and Monkey. Bowing his head, Wat Su said, "Words cannot thank you all enough for what you have done. On behalf of all my people, we salute you."

Both Dotty and the boys felt their eyes moisten and a lump rise in their throats. Monkey smiled and bowed too, before saying, "As there is no parchment, Chou Ping will perform the ritual to return you to your own time, and the bowl and chopsticks will return to us by magic. We are not sure exactly where you will reappear, but you should readjust quite quickly with no problems. We will try to make sure that no one sees you arrive."

Monkey then motioned to Tommy and John that they stand by the table, making doubly sure the chopsticks had the thicker ends touching!

Joining hands, they touched the tips as they had done before. Chou Ping started to recite the incantation, and before long they were on their way. It was hard to believe that the tingling sensation they were feeling again had been new to them only a day or so before. "Here we go kid!" said John to Tommy, as their hands started to melt into the chopsticks. Soon they had both flowed up into the bowl.

Dotty was next. She trembled slightly, but remembered to smile goodbye, as she felt herself slowly being drawn into the chopsticks and then up into the bowl. As she faded from sight Monkey mouthed a silent goodbye, and wondered whether they'd ever meet up again.

CHAPTER 29

Exeter, England

10ᵗʰ September 2001

When Mrs O'Rourke banged into the bedroom, she was amazed to find the bed still occupied, and the curtains still drawn. Dropping the clean bed linen onto the chair, she went over to the bed and gently shook the sleeping figure.

"Yes, what is it?" a drowsy voice enquired.

"It's past ten o'clock Miss, I thought you and the boys had left already!"

Dotty shook her head, her thoughts a meaningless jumble. She desperately tried to remember where she was, who this woman was, and who the boys might be.

"Where am I?" she asked.

"Why, Exeter, Miss. You and the boys booked into my B&B last night. Are you all right? Can I get you anything?"

Something stirred in Dotty's mind. Wispy thoughts of monkeys, dragons and pandas flitted through her memory then faded again. Trying hard to clear her head, she said, "Are the boys still here?"

"I don't know, Miss, I haven't checked their room yet," Mrs O'Rourke said.

Dotty tried to get up. She ached from head to toe and felt absolutely exhausted. When she managed to get the bedclothes off, she and the astonished landlady discovered that she was still fully dressed.

"Where are the boys?" she asked.

"Next room along," came the reply. Groggily she rose to her feet, went into the corridor and opened the next door. The curtains were closed too. She went to the window and drew them back.

Two heads were visible in the beds, one black haired, the other blond. She went over to the dark one and shook its owner. Tommy's face appeared, then he opened his eyes and blinked.

"Hello Auntie!" he said.

"Tommy," she said. The daylight and voices in the room had caused John to wake too. He blinked and looked at the others, trying to understand where he was and whom he was with. All of them knew something strange had happened, but try as they might, they couldn't fill the hole in their mind. Dotty was the first to give up trying to remember.

"I think we'd better leave and head home now," she said, returning to her room to get her things together. Looking in her handbag, Dotty found the car keys, and the memory of her car made itself known.

She rounded up the boys, and they made their way downstairs. It took a few minutes to locate the car, but on seeing it, both the boys seemed to relax, as another piece of their jigsaw puzzle locked together.

They got into the car and Dotty started the motor. Things were falling into place now. She remembered the boys coming down to London, but quite why they were in Exeter she wasn't sure. She realised they'd have to take a different route back, as they'd be going straight to Manchester.

Luckily, John remembered the way his father had driven back from Tidlington, and gave her directions.

Much of the journey home was spent in silence, as everyone was physically and mentally drained, and there was still a sense of unease hanging over them. Dotty drove slowly, and they stopped a couple of times on the way. Eventually they arrived home. The sight of the familiar back-to-back terraces had a soothing effect on them.

"Home sweet home!" said Tommy, and really meant it. John was equally happy to be home. Getting out of the car, he turned and waved as he crossed the road, then let himself in. Nobody was there, but his mother had left him a note telling him that his dinner was in the fridge. Wearily he headed upstairs to bed. Pulling his T-shirt off, he found a pendant on a chain round his neck. His first instinct was to take it off, but something told him to leave it where it was, so he did. He crawled under the covers, and was soon sound asleep.

THE END

POSTSCRIPT

San Francisco, USA

5th May 2003

As the clock struck eight, a man limped up and down outside the city records office, waiting for it to open. It had taken him much magic and many years to get there, but the one thing he possessed was patience. He coughed, drawing back his upper lip, exposing a set of uneven chipped and stained teeth.

He'd searched all over America, and had narrowed it down to this city. Surely, there couldn't be too many female lawyers with a Chinese name. But, even if there were, he had all the time in the world to investigate all of them. He found the crutches uncomfortable and leaned back against the granite wall of the building to ease the burden on his single leg.

He patted the stump where his other leg had been. He had a good feeling about this place.

"Don't worry. I'm coming …" he whispered.